The Lost Men
an allegory

The Lost Men
an allegory

David A. Colón

Elsewhen Press

The Lost Men
First published in Great Britain by Elsewhen Press, 2012
An imprint of Alnpete Limited

Copyright © David A. Colón, 2012. All rights reserved
The right of David A. Colón to be identified as the author of this work has been asserted in accordance with sections 77 and 78 of the Copyright, Designs and Patents Act 1988. No part of this publication may be reproduced, stored in a retrieval system or transmitted in any form, or by any means (electronic, mechanical, telepathic, or otherwise) without the prior written permission of the copyright owner. Moroni 10:3, quoted from *Book of Mormon*, 1830, Church of Jesus Christ of Latter-Day Saints, used with permission. Helen Waddell's 1929 translation of *Hymn for the Burial of the Dead* by Aurelius Prudentius, C4th AD, used with kind permission. Genesis 1:11-12, quoted from the Bible, *The New Revised Standard Version*, copyright 1989 by the Division of Christian Education of the National Council of the Churches of Christ in the United States of America. Used by permission. All rights reserved. Passage have also been quoted from the following: *Iliad*, Homer, c. C8th BC; *A Modest Proposal for Preventing the Children of Poor People From Being a Burden on Their Parents or Country, and for Making Them Beneficial to the Publick*, Jonathan Swift, 1729; *Rasselas*, Samuel Johnson, 1759; *Lines Left upon a Seat in a Yew-Tree*, William Wordsworth, 1798; *The Lifted Veil*, George Eliot, 1859. Cessna and Skyhawk are trademarks of Textron Innovations Inc. Book of Mormon is a trademark of Intellectual Reserve, Inc. Use of trademarks has not been authorised, sponsored, or otherwise approved by the trademark owners.

Elsewhen Press, PO Box 757, Dartford, Kent DA2 7TQ
www.elsewhen.press

British Library Cataloguing in Publication Data.
A catalogue record for this book is available from the British Library.

ISBN 978-1-908168-04-7 Print edition
ISBN 978-1-908168-14-6 eBook edition

Condition of Sale
This book is sold subject to the condition that it shall not, by way of trade or otherwise, be lent, re-sold, hired out or otherwise circulated in any form of binding or cover other than that in which it is published and without a similar condition including this condition being imposed on the subsequent purchaser.

This book is copyright under the Berne Convention.
Elsewhen Press & Planet-Clock Design are trademarks of Alnpete Limited

This book is a work of fiction. All names, characters, places and events are either a product of the author's fertile imagination or are used fictitiously. Any resemblance to actual events, places or people (living or dead) is purely coincidental.

Designed and formatted by Elsewhen Press

To Lucía

A morbid pleasure nourished, tracing here
An emblem of his own unfruitful life:
And, lifting up his head, he then would gaze
On the more distant scene,—how lovely 'tis
Thou seest—and he would gaze till it became
Far lovelier, and his heart could not sustain
The beauty, still more beauteous! Nor, that time,
When nature had subdued him to herself,
Would he forget those Beings to whose minds,
Warm from the labours of benevolence,
The world, and human life, appeared a scene
Of kindred loveliness: then he would sigh,
Inly disturbed, to think that others felt
What he must never feel: And so, lost Man!
On visionary views would fancy feed,
Till his eye streamed with tears. In this deep vale
He died,—this seat his only monument.

William Wordsworth, "Lines Left upon a Seat in a Yew-Tree"

One

Mann pressed, with all his might, the last red clay tile into the adhesive. The mansion beneath he affectionately knew as La Maison d'Être. Like an old dog, it from time to time needed tending to in the most humbling ways, but every embarrassing repair it suffered only added to its permanent character.

He reached for the hairdryer. Forty seconds of continuous blowing, medium heat, and the shingle is set. More would run the caulk thin: less, and it dries without bonding. He wiped his brow and sighed. For every chore the last repetition was always equally tedious and satisfying.

A ten-yard stretch on the rim of the roof was his path back. Wares in hand and five stories high, he balanced pat movements before leaping into a terrace. An hour had passed since dawn, and the clouds were pink from the new sun, and the silhouette of trees beneath was black and green and violet. Mann's vision was razor sharp; no detail of landscape was wasted on him, and he felt, as he always did, a kinship for all aspects, seen or felt, of his environs. Hues of orange were dominant, as was their warmth, in this moment of the early day—the colors of sunlight covered every surface, as real and delicate as a coat of dust.

He relished his vantage; La Maison was his city on a

hill. Barely hidden were a handful of houses, which on rare occasion he would visit to remedy his solitude. They were built with skill but empty of life, and his existence was accustomed to the void, if not defined by it.

He coiled the cord and set the dryer down under the solar collector in the corner. His rough hand gently opened a small door to the machine; he knelt, looked inside, blew at the dust, and shut the hatch. He stood to peer over the edge of the house and looked down upon twelve much larger versions of the same machine on the ground below. In geometric rows they mimicked obedience and discipline, and, like a good commander, he thought their peak performance did not excuse them from inspection but warranted it.

Through large, elegant, glass-paneled doors he stepped into the study. The denim and boots he wore contrasted sharply with the décor. On the walls hung paintings by Chagall and Kandinsky, Picasso and Miró: all taken from the homes of collectors in San Francisco and Atherton—except the late Picasso, which was in the house when he chose the residence and gave him the idea for the motif. The furniture was seventeenth-century Dutch woodwork, the built-in shelves filled with leather-bound books. *Shapes of the mind*, he thought here years ago, but now strode through with practical purpose.

He opened the accordion gate of the elevator and rode it down to the first story. The wide marble floor led him through a corridor and down a few lean steps to a roomy, well-lit kitchen. He stashed the caulk gun in a narrow closet from which he pulled a toolbox. Mediated by his presence, work and elegance were fit to complement one another. On the surface, there were contradictions, but his strength was his grace, and vice versa.

Outside smelled of freshly cut grass, the lawns embroidered with flowing stone paths. There were solar

David A. Colón

collectors to check on either side of La Maison. Mann started with those in the east. The sun powered every electrical device he used: automobile, saw, remote control, oven. Often he thought about the photoreceptive cell: who might have discovered it, first replicated it, understood its perfection.

The collectors' crowns, fans of dark rainbow-tinted panels, had an element of Kabuki Theater. He methodically examined each machine, performing the same diagnostic tests, and occasionally tightening a bolt that did not need very much tightening.

*   *

After completing the same chore in the west, he unplugged a golf cart and drove down a path into the bordering woods. He was reminded of a myth, conflated, something like trees were the reincarnated souls of warriors slain in vain—maybe the culture was an Indian tribe, or the Vikings, perhaps a topic to look into in the evening reading. Upon him came a clearing, suddenly, a din less muffled: the sounds of chickens.

His arrival generated a degree of excitement among the animals. He grabbed one of the two buckets of feed by the entrance to the enclosure, unlocked the left gate, ducked his head, and entered the cage, securing the gate behind him. Walking among the throng of roosters and chicks, his giant image was betrayed by a familial bond. Like children the birds scurried in all directions, and as he spurted kernels and grit on the ground, one hundred million years of retrospect essentially rendered them cousins.

The birds scavenged immediately. He surveyed the scene with a scrupulous eye. A rooster was shaking its head. He stepped to one of the beds against the other side of the fence and, scrutinizing a hen with concern, concluded the carbamate worked on her black mites.

Before harvesting the eggs from the hens' enclosure, he hemmed in the rooster, snagged it aflutter, and tucked it under his arm. Once outside the cage, he set down the bucket of feed, pinched the bird's face, flicked its mouth open and shut. It was as he suspected; the rooster had a crossed beak. A misshapen cranium was a defect that would be passed on to its progeny. In one unforgiving gesture, he gripped the bird's neck, pulled its vertebrae apart, and tossed it effortlessly on the knoll.

The bird ran feverishly as the eyes of its dangling neck scraped the ground. Mann went to the golf cart and opened its small trunk. He collected the eggs into a wire basket, shut the hatch, and walked after the dying rooster. He thought maybe he would stew the bird with salt and cognac for dinner. It had been a while since he opened one of the bottles he had in the cellar.

The rooster ran and ran in sightless loops. Empathy was strong in Mann and so he tried to imagine living in a body that had only moments to live, but could not. He knew, by way of his counsel, that he harbored no grave illness, and with no natural predators, at the age of thirty-three, his own death to him was the most abstract of concepts.

He grabbed the bird by the feet and laid it down on the passenger seat. He drove away and took a sudden turn toward a bright field: his garden. The expanse was two acres in size, marked by neatly ordered distinct patches of crops. He needed the seeds of a proper dish to complement his poultry stew.

As was his ritual, after parking the vehicle, he recited to himself a passage of text that took just enough time to speak before removing the first provision from the vine, Genesis 1:11-12:

> Then God said, 'Let the earth put forth vegetation: plants yielding seed, and fruit trees of every kind on earth that bear fruit with the seed in it.' And it was so. The earth brought forth vegetation: plants yielding seed of every kind, and trees of every kind bearing fruit with the seed in it. And God saw that it was good.

Upon uttering the last word, his spade unearthed a large potato, which he dusted, dropped into his basket, and piled upon two more.

The long row of lush, rough potato leaves ended, as would a waterfall, in a billow of like but lank color. He walked down the path to the bushes at the end where up close he could see the hanging bulbs, gold and vermilion; he plucked a few handfuls of *ajís dulces*, tiny shriveled peppers, from the hedge they dappled; and the heirloom tomatoes welled brightly with pride, bleeding, too, into either side of orange. The ones still shy—lime, adolescent—were left to grow some more; the rest rolled in his basket as he returned to his vehicle.

He drove a short way back before stopping in the shade of a great tree. The ground was littered with mangoes, all but a few bright and tight. He bent to pick one up, unsheathed a knife, and skillfully peeled the fruit. He remembered his childhood and missed his parents. He stared into the light as juice dripped from his chin.

*   *

The sun was well into its descent when he returned to La Maison. His legs were spotted with blood, hands blackened with grease. He stripped off all his clothes and threw them into a bin outside the back entrance. Without the slightest hint of modesty he passed naked through the kitchen, into the main hallway, up a crescent flight of stairs and through a gold-handled set of white double doors into a cavernous chamber. Its private bathroom was itself a studio, of severe angles and gray marble—centered by a recessed tub that could easily fit ten people at once. He turned two knobs and the steaming tub began to fill. To the side was a shower encased in glass doors. He entered it slowly and turned the water on. A square meter of streams rained down on his body.

He exhaled loudly. All day his skin was yoked by intentions and the needs of sustaining the body it sheltered, and as it suffered without falter the command of touch and brutality of the sun, it now unclenched the tensions of life. On the floor sat a vase of salted oil, too old to eat, with a wooden knife leaning in it. He took the knife, scooped a handful of the gritty oil, rubbed it on his arms, and recalled his Classics lessons. His father was fond of telling how Roman soldiers used to bathe in olive oil, scraping their skin clean with wooden knives, before entering the field of battle. The paste gently lathered with the black grease on his arms, and after loosening the crust with his fingernails, he peeled the filth off himself. Much, almost everything, in Mann's life was attributable to the legacy of his parents.

With the knife he scoured his entire body with more of the salted oil. When done, he turned off the shower and went to finish drawing his bath. He opened a small, wooden chest and ladled aloe extract into the tub, then added a gurgling pour of rose water, shut the box, and stepped in. For a long while he absorbed the luxurious experience, until he felt it was time to eat.

*   *

A small pot simmered on the back of the stove. The feathered, trimmed, and quartered rooster was stewing in a Dutch oven with liqueur, sea salt, and bay leaves. He put down the knife, sprinkled a pinch of dill into a bowl, and wiped his hands on a towel.

Music was playing from the salon. Since he was likely to play the piano later, he had selected one of his favorite West African recordings. He listened with the ear of a musician. One by one the instruments he followed: first the rhythm of a bass, then the syncopation of congas, the fanciful fluttering of a rattle, the peppered chords of an electric guitar. He was engrossed by the music, swept into its melody, and it escaped him to consider that actual people once performed with these instruments. While the day was a time for life, the night was a time for thought, and his evening ruminations rarely included the sentience of people he had never met.

This time, the early evening, was when he felt most alone. It was fifteen years since his parents had left him, and for seven years after that he never came in contact with another human being. He had only seen three people in his life: his parents and his counsel. He had read extensively about other people, histories of societies and conflicts, and vast collections of literature, but his sense of the human condition was comprised of a mere four first-hand accounts.

Standing under the chandelier in the salon, he put a glass to his lips and took a hearty gulp of cognac. His company was scattered eighteenth-century divans and massive oil portraits of influential men from Europe. Nothing about the subjects entered his mind; he no longer saw the paintings as documentation of people's existence but rather as demonstrations of deft handling of depth, light, and perspective. His life was lived without any consideration for anyone else, and it eluded him that his gentle dancing to Senegalese percussion, in a hall guarded by the *gens d'armes* of empire, was the slightest bit heretical by bygone standards.

The Lost Men

He swayed and moved as he felt natural. Dancing for him was effusive, directed from the inside out, not a spectacle to be regarded but simply participation with pleasure. The fact that dancing is inherently social—either to dance with a partner, in a crowd, or at least for an audience—did not exist. Nor did the styles, steps, or rules of dance: dance was not a sign but a phrase, attempts, inspiration, the innovation of feeling. He tilted his head back and welcomed the sounds of singing. A chorus of feminine voices began to repeat over and over, every bar, what he thought sounded like "*Sow, makeenow, makané!*" These words were certainly not what were said, except to Mann. That these voices were expressing meaning through their own language did not inform his experience. The only reality was his perception, and there was no measure to verify or debunk.

The syncretism of cultures endemic to his life was not novel to him. His tastes knew no national allegiance and his fluctuations of mood never discriminated against provenance. Unconsciously, and much more often than not, his actions and discretion denied such proclivities. Countries, governments, races, and borders were archaic abstractions. He personified a new dominion; the forces of the world and the extant accounts of ages past were his resources, not masters.

Thus, when he studied at night, he read with the eyes of an archaeologist. He took no ideas as maxims and never relinquished the privilege to doubt. His childhood education at the hands of his parents was intensely thorough, but having spent his entire adult life in abject solitude, he was practiced in implementing the very skills bestowed upon him to carve free every brick of psychic foundation. To him, etymology was the great myth of language; speculation, not proof, was the prime outcome of science; philosophy operated from premises protected by a species of worship; the pleasure of art was the vicarious witness of clandestine moral destruction. He was not by nature a skeptic: just conditioned by self-reliance to make meaning square with what he knew.

Off the rim of the tumbler he licked the last drop of cognac and decided that by now the stew must be ready to eat. He returned to the kitchen and turned off the stove. He put a large coaster under the simmering giblets and placed the pot into the refrigerator—this he would add to the pigs' gruel in the morning. A proper setting was prepared at the head of a large oak table, and he served himself his dinner before refilling his empty glass.

*   *

Perched on a ladder in the library, Mann was searching for another book to read. An earthquake several months before rattled La Maison enough to topple most of the 90,000 volumes stored in this room, so his recall of where books were after reshelving them was less than precise. After a minute of careful review, he dislodged a thin monograph with his index finger and tucked it, with the two others, under his arm.

He descended the ladder and walked across the room to the stairs leading up to a Baroque loft. In it were four large, comfortable couches that shared a canoe-length coffee table topped with candelabra. He placed down each in its own space: *The Lifted Veil* by George Eliot, *Rasselas* by Samuel Johnson, and a volume of *The Works of Jonathan Swift*. He had never read *The Lifted Veil*, and it was under his parents' tutelage that he read *Rasselas*, but Swift he read almost weekly. He had been working for quite some time on complete memorization of *A Modest Proposal*. For almost a year he had known by way of his counsel that his solitude was drawing to an end, so he thought it might be worthwhile someday to recite such a poignant work by rote.

Had he not read a substantial amount of commentary on the piece, he would have failed to fathom the depth of satire it intended. Mann had spent a hundred nights imagining the zeitgeist of a society so densely populated as to even conceive of the notion to cannibalize its own people. When he first looked upon *A Modest Proposal*, he was absolutely stunned; the sobriety of its decorum was so chilling that his eyes welled with tears. As a child he was nothing short of treasured, and every effort of his parents' lives was motivated to instill character and capability in their son. He was raised to survive all manner of difficulty, cultured to transport the worthiest knowledge of civilization in preparation to father his own child. Optimism may have viewed this age as the funnel in the hourglass of humanity, but to exist in a time when society had the option of feeding on itself seemed far more damned.

In spite of the critiques he subsequently reviewed, Mann's first reading of it was never fully purged. The callous details of cooking children's flesh—and of optimizing the resource by making clothes from its skin—were too vivid to be erased from his initial experience of the text. As disturbing as these images were, he found equally troubling the passage

> I grant this food will be somewhat dear, and therefore very proper for landlords, who, as they have already devoured most of the parents, seem to have the best title to the children.

This was no satire. In many ways, Mann believed, this bordered on prophecy.

David A. Colón

*   *

As was his habit, Mann began his evening reading with something new. He held *The Lifted Veil*, spread himself comfortably on one of the sofas, and opened the book to the first page:

> The time of my end approaches. I have lately been subject to attacks of *angina pectoris*; and in the ordinary course of things, my physician tells me, I may fairly hope that my life will not be protracted many months. Unless, then, I am cursed with an exceptional physical constitution, as I am cursed with an exceptional mental character, I shall not much longer groan under the wearisome burthen of this earthly existence. If it were to be otherwise—if I were to live on to the age most men desire and provide for—I should for once have known whether the miseries of delusive expectation can outweigh the miseries of true prevision. For I foresee when I shall die, and everything that will happen in my last moments.

Mann felt fortunate. He laid *The Lifted Veil* on his chest and paused to reflect on its opening. Oddly enough it spoke directly to him, for the voice seemed to combine elements of both himself and his counsel; while it suffered concern about its own well-being and future, its faculties for clairvoyance were enabled.

He could not, however, relate to the pangs of mere day-to-day life. Solitude never made him despair and he never wished for more or less than survival. The references to other people—the physician and "most men"—were, as usual, opaque. But what added most to Mann's learning was sensing the specter of death. As was commonplace in his life, what a rooster at noon could not teach him, a book at night did.

He continued to read for about an hour, gaining insight into the life of Latimer—a template for scornful relationships of indisputable proportion. But before long he came to a passage that affected him deeply. After Latimer's jealousy leads him to question the intentions of his brother's fiancée, the woman, Bertha, responds with candid vitriol:

> "What! your wisdom thinks I must love the man I'm going to marry? The most unpleasant thing in the world. I should quarrel with him; I should be jealous of him; our *ménage* would be conducted in a very ill-bred manner. A little quiet contempt contributes greatly to the elegance of life."

It was an appropriate place to stop. He put down the book, massaged his eyelids, and stood to leave the loft. His body was tinged with a nervousness he was unaccustomed to, and as he descended the steps he realized he hoped his eventual union would bring him love.

His parents certainly were in love. The exchange between Latimer and Bertha—and the disdain in Bertha for the one she was to wed—stung Mann deeply. His parents' relationship was his model for cooperation, decency, trust, and affection. There was never tension between them, never signs of disregard or ulterior, selfish motives, and their harmony bred peace, personified in their son.

But the book made him wonder. Just as Bertha played along as the content fiancée until asked the right question, was it too late to know the truth if there *was* any discord between his mother and father? Did they really love each other as deeply as their appearance evinced, or did they portray the life that needed to be preserved in the duty they performed, and that he had now inherited? Or worse, for its survival as guilt, did their love for one another stem from their mutual adoration of their son, and not from a love unconcerned with potential? As was the effect of many books he read at night, he was left searching for answers to questions from the world gone by. Plumes of filthy choices sickened the mentality of the age of population. In the face of threat, numbers expended honor, for parasitism was possible.

He briefly considered if such deceit would ever harm him. He had always assumed, though now it resembled hope, that when he met the one he would fall in love and forever be in love. His counsel never intimated that it would be otherwise, so he had harbored no doubt.

He entered the parlor. The black silhouette of the piano stood starkly before a window's iridescent view of moonlit night. Just as the book had opened his heart, he peeled back the cover of the ivory keys, and he felt his emotion sway back to the confident perch it rested on before. He sat on the velvet bench, in a darkness he never fathomed to fear, and began to touch music. With the grace of an ocean tide, his hands rolled over the board, his left exchanging between two chords, his right rearranging scales. The sounds layered sadness upon patience upon pain, until the two played as one, and they conjured faith. Without closing his eyes, he could feel his mother's fingers caress his knuckles, and he sensed his father's loyal labor in the kitchen preparing supper.

*   *

When Mann awoke in the morning, the sun was as bright as the air was silent. A bird darted past his window; he sat up and came to consciousness. Twenty minutes later he was outside churning compost, having dressed himself, eaten breakfast, and checked the barometer reading.

After tending to the livestock by mid-morning, he headed through the carport to a gravel-covered expanse. Next to an old eucalyptus tree was a sizable concrete bunker that partly hid from view a red and white single-engine Cessna Skyhawk. Like his fleet of automobiles, the airplane was connected by cables to an adjacent solar collector. He walked up to the bunker and opened its sturdy metal door. Rows of heavy steel canisters filled the space. He gripped the one closest to the door, dislodged it from its rack, and dragged the cylinder, walking backward with choppy steps, through the threshold and around to the side of the aircraft.

With great exertion he loaded the container onto the airplane. In the space that was formerly the cockpit, he had installed a carriage to hold two pesticide canisters at a time. The design enabled him to dispense the chemicals through separate detachable hoses, and he wired the airplane to receive its piloting commands by remote control from the ground.

He secured the second cylinder into position and rigged the hoses. Returning to the bunker, he removed from the wall the portable remote control console, unplugged it, walked outside and disconnected the cables attached to the underbelly of the plane. He backed away from the vehicle, his eyes fixated on its form, and flipped a switch that fired the piston that made the propeller begin to turn. The vibrating noise was violent and powerful. It was the loudest thing he had ever heard, beside thunder.

Using his thumbs to manipulate two miniature joysticks, he made the plane roll forward and turn gradually to its left. He stood directly behind it and aligned its body with the runway ahead. There was no wind to account for; the trees were perfectly still, the smattering of clouds a portrait. He pushed two more buttons and the plane sped forward. Its wheels crunched over gravel until it took to steady flight.

Once the aircraft climbed to adequate height, he pressed a button to engage the autopilot. He had programmed this feature to include the coordinates of the circular flight path as well as the timed commands to release the pesticides. His purpose was to spray a ring of the chemicals around the perimeter of land he used. The length of this diameter was about thirty miles, so the duration of the flight was approximately fifteen minutes.

He stood and watched the plane in the sky tilt and turn to its left. Within seconds the craft opened its right valve and started releasing the mist. He carefully watched the plane circle overhead until it passed out of sight behind the highest nearby hill.

He waited patiently for its return. The minutes elapsed as the specifics of further tasks entered his mind; he was sorting the logistics of what was capable of being accomplished today. Three minutes passed, and then five, and he grew curious. The plane should have made its pass around the hill by this point but it was not visible. Seven minutes passed, and then ten. His concern grew. The slightest malfunction could cause the plane to be lost. Eleven, then twelve, and he felt his face tense. Thirteen, and then sixteen, and by eighteen he knew that something was very wrong.

In disbelief he waited until twenty-five minutes had expired. Total silence confirmed that the airplane was no longer with him. The charge from the solar collector guaranteed only thirty minutes of flight time, but even if the plane came immediately into view, the time it would take to position and guide it into landing might exceed that window of opportunity. This was a risk he would not take; a crash could decimate the carport, or even La Maison.

The Lost Men

Resigned to pragmatism, he raised the remote control, deactivated the autopilot and shut down the engine.

He returned to La Maison in dismay. The catastrophe meant he would need to procure a new Cessna from the hangar at Moffett Field, and outfitting it the way he had before could take weeks, even months. He contemplated existing without the pesticide drop, comforting himself with the idea that maybe it was not completely necessary after all.

*   *

It was noontime and so he decided to prepare a lunch. Rather than eat raw food, he cooked to soothe his frustration. In a short time a rabbit was stewing in a sauce of tomatoes and peppers. He opened a cupboard to remove a porcelain bowl when he thought he heard a motion outside. His attention was aroused, every sense drawn together, and he walked with anticipation to the entrance behind the dining table.

A tall, stout woman appeared outside the windows and approached the doors. His face was lax with recognition, and he cleared his throat to speak for the first time in a long while.

She opened the doors and looked him in the eyes.

"Hello, Mann," she warmly greeted him.

"Hello, Joy," he happily responded.

She pulled a chair out from the table and gently sat down. "Are you well?"

"I am, thank you. The land is doing quite well, and my readings of late have been extraordinarily gratifying. But today I suffered a significant impediment." He looked down and then up. "In the pesticide run, I lost the Cessna."

"I know," she replied forgivingly. "This is in part why I

am here."

Mann was intrigued, but not so as to be impolite. "I'm cooking; would you like to eat with me? With *this* aroma, you wouldn't decline the offer."

"Thank you, Dear, I'll join you. And I'm sure it smells delicious." She smiled softly.

He returned to the cupboard and removed two bowls. "So you know the fate of the airplane?"

"Indeed I do."

"What came of it?"

Her expression grew grave. "There was no malfunction, nor an accident of any kind."

Her pause concerned him.

"The plane was taken down. This was the doing of another man."

His skin flushed with panic.

"Are you *sure?*" His voice cracked. Joy had spoken of such men—the hidden, the hateful, the remorseless—only twice in the better part of a decade. He pursed his lips to say something else, but froze in thought as her words registered in his mind.

"Yes."

"*Here?* Around *here?*"

"He is in the hills and used a weapon to destroy your plane. But I want you to know that he poses no further danger to you."

"How so?"

"He's not well, and won't live for much longer."

"Why do you say this?"

"If he were well, and capable, he would not have taken down your plane but tracked it to this home and saved his force to kill you, not the machine."

"How can you be sure?"

"That is what lost men do," she answered with gentle confidence.

The Lost Men

"But what if he thought I was piloting the plane?"

"A lost man does not take extensions of life but life itself. Destroying your plane was a desperate and misguided effort on his part. His energies are weakened, his mind clouded with demise. I know he is close to dying, and I will soon seek him out to confirm his passing."

Mann stared blankly into space, squinted his eyes and wondered. He believed Joy wholeheartedly, as he always did and knew to do, but the shock of this report was worrisome to the extreme.

"I need to know," he said to her, "how certain you are of this event and its outcome."

"I am certain."

He placed napkins on the table and set spoons on top of them. His conduct poorly masked his fear. He asked, "Is this something you intuited, or have you envisioned this?"

Without raising her eyes, she replied, "A counsel does not distinguish between the two."

Two

In the forest of a valley damp and lush, a woman hiked briskly as a man loyally followed. The wilderness bore no marks of human trespass; trees spired to darken the ground; some rocks were covered with moss of a toxic green. There were no flowers, and decay was in the process of death giving birth. The terrain was everywhere uneven.

Faith calculated each boot's step. Her staff was hooked on the top like a shepherd's, which she used occasionally to snag a branch or root and pull herself up an especially steep incline. Paine was twenty years older but of equal constitution and reliable. They betrayed a synergy of existence, and their purpose was strong and silent.

They were almost there. Their backpacks were stuffed with equipment and about six pounds of elderberries each.

"*Ow!*" she blurted and jerked up her knee.

"What is it?"

She swiftly turned, revealing a rattlesnake pinned down. "It bit me. Take it."

Paine clubbed the snake's head and held it under his staff. Faith dropped to the ground and pulled up her pant leg. The bite left two holes, one smaller than the other. The mark was not bleeding, and as she removed her belt from her waist she commanded, "Give me yours."

Paine unfastened his belt with his free hand, pulled it

loose and tossed it to her. It was almost unreal. He had not forecast Faith's demise, so the two subconsciously knew that she would not die from this ordeal. But a failure to react to the reality of the situation could mean that this event, potentially tragic, was not meant to be anticipated. The living assumption of predestination that ruled their lives was an elusive force. It was equally true that actions defined fate and fate defined actions.

Faith pressed the tip of a blade right next to the larger hole. The muscles in her jaw flexed visibly as she clenched the pain, and she similarly stabbed the other entry mark.

Paine spoke sheepishly, nervously. "I would suck the poison out for you if only I could taste it."

"I know you would, and I know you can't," she replied. "But venom doesn't taste like anything, Paine."

"Oh, then, well..." he started, but tailed off as he saw her put her lips to the wound.

She sucked audibly, spat, sucked again, then spat, the largest vein in her neck growing prominent. "I'm not getting any fluid," she announced. She resumed and her confidence grew. There were signs that the bite was not dangerous; since the wound was not bleeding much, her blood had not been thinned by venom. More than that, though, she did not feel the snake's poison. Faith was well attuned to sense and touch, and she would have known if her body was invaded by a mercenary intent.

Paine still stood with the snake under his staff. He rolled it gently back and forth to see if it could move, then clubbed its head several times more until satisfied it was dead. He knelt before it, removed his knife and gouged its underside. The opening came apart. He probed. Inside he discovered a well-preserved mouse. So *this* was why it felt vulnerable yet deposited no venom. Nothing was to die that was not supposed to die, and Paine's pride was immediately restored.

*   *

Faith was heaping more kindling on the fire when night fell. From a spit hung a pot of simmering fruit. The camp consisted of a trailer, a cabin tent, and the pyre.

"Mmm...cumquat *is* pretty good, but I'd still take whippersnapper, peccadillo, or sarsaparilla. Or hemoglobin. Or jambalaya. Or oleaginous. Or fart."

Paine chuckled almost reluctantly, though the levity was welcome.

"Boy, Paine, this sure is going to taste good," she exclaimed as she held a rod, tipped with blackened flesh, to the fire. "D'you remember when we used to eat snake all the time?"

"When?"

"When we were in Atlanta," she replied.

Paine nodded. The swampland returned to his mind.

She took her skewer from the flame. "Not like Chicago, though. The Windy City...D'you remember the museum there?"

Paine reminisced. "Yes, I do."

Faith's eyes were placed deeply in recall. "So *pristine*."

Paine felt irony. And whenever he felt a strong sense of the unspoken, the discussion would often veer. His ability to foresee certain events commonly accelerated their dialogues. There were many moments in speaking with him that could only be described as at once backtracking and leaping ahead, an environment that had, over the years, exercised Faith's acumen. This time, however, the conversation kept its course.

"The measure of a civilization's worth is the art it holds in esteem, wouldn't you say?"

Paine snickered softly. "I thought it was the art it

The Lost Men

produced," he replied.

She put her skewer back to the flame. "Not in the modern world, Paine."

The two looked to the fire to cleanse their palate of disagreement. The burning wood fizzed and crackled, as if a well-mannered third party voicing a change of subject.

After some silence Paine spoke. "I distinctly remember the Asian collection."

"Really? In Chicago?"

"Yes. I vividly recall a statue. There was a statue there of a Bodhisattva." They shared a confident glance. "He was sitting on an hourglass pedestal with his head listing to the side in repose; the expression captured at once his serenity, humility, and prolonged suffering."

"I wasn't there with you," Faith said. "We parted ways in that museum."

"Did we?"

"Sure we did. What I remember—let's see: El Greco's Assumption of the Virgin. Grand and dark, too dark. *Oh!*—and Gauguin's painting of the girl..." she tailed off restlessly, "with the eyebrows..." She gestured to herself, snapping her fingers. "The Ancestors painting. The girl from Tahiti."

Paine knew both paintings. He ignored her pause by smirking at the comparison.

"The colors were beautiful. Oh, and the self-portrait of Van Gogh." She took her skewer from the flame, blew on it, began waving it gently. "There was another painting...I *think* it was in Chicago...by Picasso, all gray with hints of rust. It was an abstraction of a man, I think it was called Henry-David something or other—I can't recall the name." She pushed some gravel. "But it was so...in the mind's eye of Picasso."

Paine's brow was arched. "You remember this fondly."

She nodded and took a small bite of the meat on her

stick, chewing with a glistening of grease on her lips.

"This is all so very telling," Paine continued. "I had no idea you were such a fan of portraiture."

Faith's eyes darted, and she replied, "Well, the Assumption is not a portrait."

"Sure it is. I *was* there with you, and I remember these paintings, too. The Assumption has other characters, but it's basically a portrait of the Virgin Mary, and undoubtedly the other three paintings you recall are portraits."

Faith stopped to think.

"Are these portraits the only paintings that stand out to you in this memory?"

Faith pondered. "Yes, actually, I think they are."

"What do you think this means?"

"What do you mean *what do you think this means*?"

"What I mean is do you think this is revealing of anything? What captivates you so about the image of the individual?"

"I'm not sure." She took another bite of meat.

He patiently waited for her to speak again. After ten seconds of expanding tension, she swallowed aggressively. "It must be a reflection of my own inflated, narcissistic over-appreciation of self."

Her snideness was overblown, and yet it was obvious she practically read his mind. "Careful not to speak the truth into being," he remarked, almost whispering.

Her head tilted dramatically, her demeanor turned cold. "Paine, how many people have you known in your life?"

"Six," he answered without hesitation.

"And of those six, how many of them are still alive?"

"One."

"And in what capacity do you know this person?"

"She is you, and I know you because I am your counsel."

"And why are you my counsel?"

"To aid you in fulfilling your destiny."

Although these truths were never far from either's mind, speaking the words felt heavy: a dire strain, a stillbirth.

She nodded facetiously. "That's all?"

He said nothing.

"For the seven years we've ranged this continent we haven't met another *soul*. Considering all things, don't you think that maybe, just maybe, it wouldn't be too grave a sin to have admiring tastes? Discriminating tastes? Of fine art? In *fact*, don't I have an *obligation* to do so?!"

"I didn't mean to rile or offend you."

"But you *did*," she said as she stood up. She paced a few steps in a circle, then snapped her skewer in two and hurled the pieces at the fire. "Well, what difference does it make," she resigned. "There are no artists anymore."

*   *

After cleaning up and smothering the fire, Paine followed Faith to the tent. Inside was lit by an old fashion kerosene lamp.

"Are you alright?" he gingerly asked.

"Of course I'm alright," she replied, "I just don't understand your intentions. For a simple, heartfelt recollection you attacked me; that really was unwarranted."

"I beg to differ."

"Why? I was simply remembering some art pieces we saw. You and I both know that art is vital to humanity, and it's something that should be preserved and remembered and passed on, and hopefully revived."

"I agree."

"And this idea I've been sensing in you lately that I harbor hubris and an inflated sense of self is not only uncalled for but misdirected. Why are you choosing now to profess this lesson of humility?"

"Now in your maturity I think it is vital. Just as valuing art is important to preserve and instill in future generations, a foundation of modesty is central to any semblance of ethics."

Faith was at a loss for words. She succumbed to a sense that she was right but that Paine was also right. Thus she was receptive to more words of moral concern—and Paine knew it. He reached out and caressed her hand for a moment, then sat up straight and crossed his legs. On occasion, he spoke in parables when they were faced with conflict or one of his uncertain, bleak visions.

He said, "I will tell you a tale that my father once told me.

"In a beautiful grove stood a full-blossomed peach tree, more brimful and magnificent than all the others. It was the season of life, and all the fruit were fragrant and luscious with juice and water and flavor.

"A young monkey, eager to have his fill of the bountiful fruit, chose this most abundant tree and hopped up into its canopy. Every peach was ripe and enticing: plump, soft to the touch, and colored with pink and streaks of gold. He reached to pluck one, when another peach spoke: 'Dear monkey, do you not see me hanging here on the strongest branch? Of all the peaches in this tree, I am the most perfect. My skin is tight, my flesh is soft, my juice is sweet and ready to quench. There is no other more desirable than me, and having me will bring you only the greatest of satisfaction.'

"The peach spoke with a vanity that belied its intention. It praised itself only because it was eager to ensure that its seed would be cast to the earth and grow into a magnificent tree itself. The peach longed to realize its purpose, to partake in the cycle of life and prosper as every being finds necessary.

The Lost Men

"The young monkey was easily persuaded, picked the fruit and bit into it. The peach was as delicious as it had claimed, and the monkey delighted in the luxury of eating such a perfect fruit. So excited and inspired was the monkey that he fled the grove and returned to the jungle as quickly as he could to share the news of his experience with his family.

"The young monkey gathered the others and, in animated fashion, told the story of eating the most delectable fruit ever known. The others were fascinated by his account, trusting every word of his passionate tale, for the young know little of conviction, and even less of deceit.

"When his elders lamented the fleeting nature of such bliss, the young monkey offered a token of repair: 'Here is the pit of that divine fruit. I hold in my hand the core of that treasure for all to behold, and never to be forgotten.' At once the peach pit was placed in the highest nook of the highest tree, guarded and explained generation after generation, forever to be exalted as an object too sacred to release: to plant, grow, and impugn to mortality.

"For one hundred years the pit rested in the crown of the jungle, until one day an old sloth discovered it nestled in its lofty perch. The pit addressed the sloth: 'Dear sloth, you must wonder how a peach pit finds itself placed so high above the jungle. I am the pit of the most delicious fruit ever known, enjoyed by an ape that found my flesh to be so perfect that I have become the treasured relic of his clan. For a century the monkeys have revered my legacy. But now I ask you to do with me what would be most befitting one of my precious nature.'

"Once again, the pit spoke with a vanity that belied its intention. It narrated its history only because it was eager to ensure that its seed would be cast to the earth and grow into a magnificent tree itself. The pit longed to realize its purpose, to partake in the cycle of life and prosper as every being finds necessary.

"The old sloth heeded the words it spoke, and deliberately caressed the pit into its claws. It had been too long since the rains were plentiful, and all the animals had since hoped for a fierce monsoon to replenish the jungle with bounty from the vine. The old sloth climbed down to a branch that hung above a river, tossed the pit into the water, and said: 'River, take this cherished gift, and hear my wish: may the rains return and bear the blossoms that sustain us all, and bring us life.'

"Soon the clouds swirled darkly in the sky, and the rains came with thunderous force. The river flowed faster, its banks raised, and the pit drifted downstream as the torrent raged behind it. The river cast the pit out to the ocean, the rush shuttling it through the jagged coral reef, where its shell cracked and fell, releasing its seed. In the ocean the seed drifted for one hundred years, until it floated into a duct along the coast of a faraway land.

"One day a farmer, planting rice, discovered the seed lodged in the mud. He picked it up, wiped it clean, and determined that it was from no tree he had ever known. 'Seed,' the farmer wondered, 'how did you get here? There are no trees of your kind here, nor ever have been. Tell me of the travels you have weathered; you must be an omen of greatness.'

"With the wisdom of two centuries of reflection, it replied, 'I am a seed, like any other. I was born into flesh, and cast onto fate.'

"The farmer was satisfied with such a simple answer. He put the seed into his pocket and walked uphill to his tiny home. He placed the seed inside a teacup, set it next to his bed, and kept it until the end of his days as a reminder of the value of humility."

The Lost Men

*   *

When Paine finished, they remained silent for a minute.

She spoke. "I think I understand."

His response was a stare.

"My true destiny, in its entirety, is unfathomable. And my kismet in life is independent of my will."

He nodded. "And thus...?"

She replied, "And thus there's a problem."

"What is it?"

"The moral of this fable is that a resignation to the power of fate, masked as modesty, is the safest way to reconcile will with the unforeseen."

Paine responded, "It's not safety; it's truth."

"It's a lie," Faith retorted. "Only action, willful action, breeds fate. Fate cannot exist without will. And in the face of consequences with potentially dire outcomes, the urgency of will must be grounded in confidence."

Paine began to speak, but Faith interrupted.

"I have accepted that destiny reveals itself to you in stages, and from time to time," she continued, "and I accept that I cannot fathom it altogether without uncertainty. But my own determination to realize the mark of my own life is as potent a force as any, and beyond that it is perhaps the most important value to be preserved in humanity. I *do* want to live, and I *do* want to survive, and I *do* want to bear a child and raise it to maturity because I feel both a love and an obligation to do so, and I won't exist as one who feels no conviction either way. This is both reasonable and primal: both a strategy and a reflex. And you know what Paine? You aren't immune to this passion."

Paine was surprised. "What are you insinuating?"

"All this began with your own recollection of the art we witnessed in Chicago. Do you remember what piece you said you found so striking?"

"The Bodhisattva."

"And why?"

"For its expression of humility, and..."

"So the life of the Bodhisattva," she interjected, "*coincidentally* mirrors your own? The Bodhisattva was a man who postponed his own quest for enlightenment in order to help others attain *their* enlightenment. He was a guide, a *counsel*, Paine, exactly like you. Now I suppose you'll tell me that in no way were you projecting *your* own sense of self-worth upon that statue you found so powerful, but I won't be convinced. Nor would I blame you—in fact, I'd commend you for it."

Paine remained silent.

"That was an entertaining parable, one I won't soon forget, but I have my own anecdote to share with you: 'Be not too hasty to trust or to admire the teachers of morality. They discourse like angels, but they live like men.'"

Paine looked her in the eyes. "Who wrote that?"

"Samuel Johnson," she replied. "Offering advice to a *prince*."

The conversation was ended. She put out the lamp, they lay down, and their breathing slowed before they fell asleep.

*   *

A dream. A restful feeling. A passing through darkness. A sense of the body. A position lying prone, facing up. A touch surrounding the skin with motion. A complete immersion in what feels like hands. A growing sensation, being engulfed by writhing, living things. A realization of the serpentine nature swirling tightly all around. A panic: the touches grow less benign and increase in speed. A cold, hard, black plane touches from below and pushes

The Lost Men

gently up. A patient moving through the layered strands upward to the surface. A cleansing light upon emerging from the infinite, slithering pool. A view of the orange sky and wispy clouds. A sun that grows smaller and changes shape. A sunflower's blossom, extending down into view. A black core within yellow petals. A closer view, growing bigger. A bloody, shriveled pit. A rotten seed. A horror.

* *

Faith awoke terrified. Her nightmare lingered, for a moment, until she saw the inside of the tent and exhaled. She sat up, licked her lips, and pulled on her eyelashes.

Outside, Paine finished packing up the camp and was ready to collapse the tent. When Faith emerged he wished her a good morning, then told her of a town a few miles away in which to hunt, restock supplies, and clean her wound.

They drove up a cleared path that intersected with a paved road: a narrow, winding stretch of what was once an interstate highway. She proceeded with eyes attentive to potential roadblocks as it wound and curved through the powerful wilderness. As always, they moved ahead while arching back, feinting returns to the past that never quite materialized.

The asphalt path was a seam through nature. Flat and carefully engineered, the trail of carbon solder scarred the plush fabric of forest. But time had healed the wound some; the road was littered with seeds and leaves fallen from a thin canopy that hid the groove from the heavens. The road was more like a tunnel, and the two inched the miles of its scale like a maggot wriggling through flesh.

The artery straightened. In a short time they came upon ruins of human life: a roofless barn, a peeling billboard, a tractor with flowers growing from its gearshift. The further they entered into the dead cell, the more preserved were the core remains of civilization. It was as though the planted roots of humanity made its ground less inhabitable for other living things.

They were the first people to pass through the town in almost two centuries. Up and down Main Street, pigeons fluttered in and out of glassless windows, the road lined with brown mounds of rust, the storefronts retaining hints of foregone purpose. She drove slowly as they surveyed the scene. They passed a tax attorney's office, a dance studio, a bar. A pharmacy, a diner, an antiques shop. A transcript of bygone needs lay before them, but it was no matter.

What they sought was a house by a lake. Paine directed Faith to a driveway on the outskirts of town. At the end of the silt path was a large Colonial home. They exited the vehicle, gathered necessary belongings, and entered the front door.

Despite the cobwebs, the home was entirely livable. Unlike Faith, Paine knew that this home had passed, for generation after generation, down a long line of survivors. Its inhabitants had cared for it well.

They inspected the residence for its assets: kitchenware, mirrors, weatherproof apparel. After taking inventory of the space, she left through the back entrance, as Paine stood and stared with curiosity at the television screen in the family room.

Behind the house was a lake, tranquil and still save the narrow fluttering of innocuous waves by the shore. Faith stripped naked and bathed in the cold water, scrubbing herself with liquid soap and a patch of terry cloth. Frothy clumps of bubbles floated on the surface around her. She plunged into the water to rinse her body clean, then emerged erect to leave the lake swathed in a newness and beauty reminiscent of Venus.

The Lost Men

*   *

Alone, she returned from the hunt at dusk and saw a stream of smoke ascending from the chimney. Slung over her shoulder was a noose holding three dead geese. Her other hand gripped a warm shotgun.

She removed her long boots before entering the house. Inside, lamps were lit and kindling blazed in the fireplace. Paine was nowhere to be found so she began to prepare the game by herself.

When he returned, the roasting geese were hanging from twine in front of the fire. Faith, dressed in soft clothing, was lying in her sleeping bag on the floor reading a book. Paine passed through another part of the house. She could hear him walk up the stairs and down the hallway. It was often that they minded themselves in spite of their reliance. She needed time to think and to remember; he needed patience to make sense of the future.

Lately the future seemed smaller. For many years Faith had lived under the dominion of a future that felt practically endless, but the space of that universe was noticeably shrinking. At the moment it felt neither good nor bad, though these emotions wavered leading up to now. Sometimes this sense felt constricting, like being buried in a box running out of air. Other times it felt like a slow, gentle embrace of love that kept her standing when fallen weak.

Presently she had reconciled these extremes. Her responsibility to humankind was not at odds with her passions. She had envisioned myriad futures for herself, all with distinct outcomes tracing unique life courses right up to her death, and was psychically prepared to meet any of these fates. Most days she invented a new one and stored it in her mind to augment her ability to live in spite of nature's conspiracies contesting her survival.

David A. Colón

As she matured she had grown more and more optimistic. It could not be said that she was ever dour or frightened, but nonetheless experience only added to her composure and faith. She bolstered this stance with readings of religious nature, for she thought that humanity's quest for eternal life was proof of its inspiring powers. Spiritual doctrines, she believed, confirmed the essential need for optimism. She had read the Koran, the Talmud, the Torah, and the Bible, and before her lay the Book of Mormon. In her mind, it was not just Buddhism but every religion's quest to assuage suffering and privilege the works of kindness, and this ethic reigned supreme over her own pitiable life. Rapt by these sentiments, she read from Moroni 10:3:

> Behold, I would exhort you that when ye shall read these things, if it be wisdom in God that ye should read them, that ye would remember how merciful the Lord hath been unto the children of men, from the creation of Adam even down until the time that ye shall receive these things, and ponder it in your hearts.

She reflected on the prescience of these words. She could not imagine an age in which humanity was posed a graver threat than now, but since she herself believed in the mercy of fate, the prophet's plea was never more pertinent and alive.

Her meditation was interrupted as Paine entered the room. He slowly walked past the fire and into the dining nook. With his back turned to her, he said her name.

"What is it?" she replied. "Are you ready to eat? I think these are done." She walked to the fireplace, cut down the geese, and placed them on the tray set beneath them. She brought them to the dining table, but something in Paine's demeanor caught her attention.

The Lost Men

"Sit down," he told her.

She paused, then yielded, pulled out a chair and sat. She was unnerved. "What is it?" she repeated.

Paine looked down, then at the wall, then at her. His gaze was forceful and possessed of honesty. "There's something I have to tell you."

Three

The spoons clinked in the bowls as Mann placed them in the sink. He felt better after talking with Joy; he trusted her to know and do what was in his best interest. The stove was no longer on and the pot was no longer hot, though the kitchen was warmer.

"Come here, Dear," his counsel said. "So much talk of grave matters needs remedy."

Mann returned to the table and sat down. "Don't worry. I know what you say. But you can understand my dread of the lost man."

"I certainly can, but that is no longer of consequence. However, something else is."

"Yes?"

"I told you that news of your plane is only *in part* why I am here."

Mann's hands, unaccustomed to idleness, were restless, so he rubbed his knuckles together. "That's right, you did," he replied, and looked at her.

She beamed with anticipation. His hands stopped moving. He sensed one of those great moments that words alone can affect, but never contain.

He began nervously, "Are you going to..."

"*Shhhhhh*," she responded gingerly, for all his questions were soon to be dashed. "Mann, my precious dear:

"*The one has become apparent to me.*"

The Lost Men

His world dissolved at the words.

With a whisper the woman sealed his fate.

He pushed himself from the table and stood. The chair tipped and fell with a loud crack. He walked through the kitchen, dragging his fingers on any surfaces in reach, his eyes wide open and looking at nothing. Joy might have said something more. His senses ceased to inform as he wandered slowly into the salon, and his counsel eventually followed.

Her words returned to him: "The one has become apparent to me." It could be said that his whole life, every aspect of his creation and existence, was intended to receive this message, and he knew this deeply. In ways, he knew it almost too well, its charms of hope and sedation: more a will o' the wisp than a beacon. Up to the moment of his counsel's announcement, he had been deluded of his connection to the reality of his life. Unwittingly, he had been living in a realm of potential, an extended dress rehearsal for the performance of his destiny.

But he realized that nothing could have changed this. Fate's way was to perpetually render the moment imaginary; looking ahead to promises of fruition evacuated the present of any autonomous charge of meaning. All he could do before, he pondered, was pretend gravity, and do so in the most realistic manner possible. In this regard, he was a dutiful subject.

What he pretended, pertaining to the one, was scavenged from his scant experiences with the people he had known. Desire took the fore when regarding the one, and he harvested desire mainly from his mother. Her smell, her touch, her face: patchwork woven into his image of the one, for he believed as many before him believed that desire was a requisite for love. His mother was his model for an object of desire and much of his reading justified this; in fact, his reading was his inspiration. He never naturally desired his mother in a passionate way, but since so many books had elaborated on Freud's theory—the inherent urge to covet one's mother—he took their inductive claims to deduce his own purpose of devotion, for otherwise the portrait of the one in his anticipating mind would have been an empty canvas.

Perplexity ebbed as surroundings returned to him. The fixity of objects and their density became apparent—the floor, the walls, the hanging paintings—and their certitude of existence buttressed his momentarily frail sanity. With his retreat into attention came the re-emergence of his counsel.

She sat on a sofa. "Are you not pleased?"

Still standing, he turned to her. "Well, yes, I am...I mean, of course I am."

"But understandably befuddled..."

"Certainly," he responded. "I myself sensed no indication that the one was so near."

She blinked slowly and smiled. "Well, she is."

He turned around in a complete circle. "I...I just don't know. I just don't know if I'm ready."

"Surely you are, for if you weren't, then she wouldn't be, either."

To one blindly faithful to the power of destiny, this notion was an empirical truth. But Mann doubted. "How can you be so sure?"

"How can one *not* be?" she responded lightly.

The point was made. This was undeniable; readiness could only be initiated by need, by advent, by impending change. He could never be ready for the one until he was called upon to receive her, and being summoned as such was the only necessary qualification.

*   *

The Lost Men

The two were sitting in the salon.

"And so the image is strong?" he asked.

"Indeed," she replied. "Far more so than any inklings aligned in the past."

Mann adjusted his sitting position. "So...tell me what I don't know."

"She is prepared to begin her quest for you," Joy began. "She will arrive in three days with her counsel."

Mann started to piece together the truth of his fate. The visage of his mother was still present in his mind.

"Her journey has been difficult. She is nomadic, inclined to gather and hunt for her survival rather than do as you have done in establishing your home."

Mann continued to envision his mother. She, too, was a wanderer before meeting his father.

"As such, she has seen much of the world. She is well read—her parents took the same care that yours did in cultivating the young mind—and maintains intellectual habits, but much of her education has come from firsthand experience of architecture, art, scenery, and terrain. She reads the world as she reads books and has vast stores of information ready to hand, ones you should find intriguing and worthwhile."

This, too, was in line with his account of his mother. Perhaps more so than his father, his mother was the great teacher in his life. She had survived varied climates and was competent and resourceful in both rural and urban environments, and the diversity of her experience served her well as a parent in a world bereft of security.

To imagine the one, books completed that which the memory of his mother could not. *Is the one to be as beautiful as Helen? Could she be as impetuous as Caroline Lamb? Is she as indignant as Olympe de Gouges? Is her virtue as profound as Saint Teresa, or more like Guinevere?* The impossibility of knowing could not dissuade him from prognosticating. He was a man, and for every concocted precept of femininity was an earnest hope for perfection of character. Until meeting the one, he would remain with one foot in the domain of speculation, for not only was he dreaming of the unknown but many traits he wished for in her were yet to be realized in her own, real life. Just as he was unready before this brusque initiation, so were many of her merits untested and hence immaterial.

Then Joy said something that collided with his vision. "I cannot offer a complete picture of the one, though in the days to come more will be revealed to me. But I can say this, and with certainty: she is fiercely strong and kind of heart."

At this moment the image of his mother was shattered. Preserved, with some exaggeration, at the core remembrance of his mother were, in his estimation, her two greatest flaws. Mature and in retrospect, he concluded her strength was extrinsic; his father was the source of the family's fortitude whenever doubt, fear, or threat crept upon them. In the years of famine his father provided assurance in both forms of encouragement and industry. He would forgo sleep to hunt for days on end, and when Mann fell gravely ill to a virus as a child, it was his father who nursed his health—while his mother failed to conceal her despair. When times were hard, she vanished it seemed, and every memory Mann had of crisis was marred: by his mother's concession, and his father's undue stoicism.

And though doubtlessly maternal, she nevertheless tended to be less than kind. Her want of true kindness, of the sort that exuded pity or selfless compassion, was tied to her weakness. Mann believed she invested so much feeling in raising him that whenever her efforts were jeopardized by nature's cruelty, she emotionally fled and took to pessimism. He decided she had no faith in destiny, intermittently resorting to a defense mechanism of distancing herself from the ones she loved in order to stay one step ahead of a callous fate.

None of this expensed his love for her. After all, she was once a child, too, and her self was equally molded by the circumstances of her own subjective upbringing. Mann had many years to reflect on these notions, and he knew that mortality had its identifying markings: fear had many faces, and was as real as anything in life. *The greatest wisdom is always pithy: to err is human, to forgive, divine.*

His counsel continued, "She is greatly in need of you. She has endured her solitude with enviable dignity but nonetheless has relied on her hopes of you as much as you have of her. She loves what the promise of you has represented and is equally ready to receive you and love you without reservation."

Mann was humbled. "This is very auspicious."

"Indeed it is," she replied, satisfied with his honesty. Although Joy had visions of the one, she had not foreseen Mann's reaction to this news. After a moment's pause, she added, "Preparations must be made for her arrival."

"Certainly," he quickly replied. "I've thought of this a great deal. Do you have any instructions for me as I prepare to receive her?"

"No, I have none. Now is the time for me to defer to *your* vision of the future," she intimated with some felicity.

He looked at her with round eyes, raised his brow and smiled. "Well it's about time!" he said loudly, and they both laughed.

The two sat in happy silence for several moments, perhaps even a minute. They made eye contact and smiled again.

"My dear," Joy said, "there is something else, though it shouldn't come as a surprise."

"Yes?"

The counsel put her hands on her knees and said, "She is fertile."

Mann was not surprised, though relieved. For a moment the image of his mother returned to his mind.

*   *

That afternoon he began his preparations for the one. He vigorously cleaned several rooms in La Maison and refreshed the decorations. He wrote lists on paper of unusual chores—to cut flowers, to polish shoes, to rehearse recitation of *A Modest Proposal*. He browsed his wardrobe and put together outfits, shaved his neck and composed elaborate menus. The next few days would be unavoidably restless and so he promised himself to be as productive as he could.

Yet as human as the impending events seemed, the driving force behind them was entirely animalistic. He functioned almost unconsciously, as if by primordial trance—it was a mating ritual of elaborate detail never taught but intuited. His behavior was a distinct blend of instinct and culture; the urge was to display, the signs discreetly chosen.

*   *

After Mann and Joy parted ways, the counsel left La Maison and embarked on her search for the lost man. She traveled by foot as she always did. From various closets and compartments she had gathered necessities into a backpack before starting out on her hike.

She left La Maison pondering Mann's emotional

The Lost Men

wellbeing; he seemed perplexed at first upon hearing her prophecy, and that concerned her. She had hoped he would have felt overjoyed. The fact that his instinctive response was essentially apprehensive was an omen she was not ready to forget.

She thought many thoughts about him, as always. Her mind was perpetually consumed by him; for years now his needs were her life. When alone, as she was nearly all the time, visions of varied levels of reality—past, present, future, possibility—flickered in her mind, visions all of him. She caught glimpses of him as a father, saw him ill, imagined his passing, moments precipitating unconcerned for her own awareness, self, concentration, or will. As a counsel, her identity could never be thought of as in any way fixed, or even, truly, her own. She was less than a person but more than an individual, with more than one force paving the course of her inward existence. Trains of thought were circuitous and tangential, unpredictable and forever tugging her sense of reason in unfamiliar directions.

But, carefully sorted, the confusion was empowering. She had for a long while been accustomed to this language through which fate communicated with her, with its awkward idiom and inflected timing. As time passed and she aged, her understanding of fate's expression grew less grammatical and more fluent. She could direct its motives more.

At present her motive was to find the lost man. She left La Maison from the rear and headed south toward the hills, passing the threshold of the wilderness in a short time. Her path paralleled the bordering areas Mann cultivated for farming. A mere hundred yards away, carefully patterned rows of identical plants grew with a purpose beyond their nature, but under her feet and over her head the forest was unclaimed by man. She marveled subconsciously at the difference, suppressing a sort of disgust with the subtle perversion rendered by agriculture, as if the right angles of his planted crops were akin to a six-legged toad.

This reminded her of the lost man. She thought that the will people impose on nature was somehow consanguine with murder. It had to be; she still had no way of explaining why lost men existed except by considering them as reconfigurations of basic human instincts. Mann was pure, natural, and harmonious with existence. On the other hand, the lost man was purposeful in calculating a dramatic effect on the living world around him, expensing all else at his own curious, even vile, discretion—like acres of tilled soil. *Mann, the forest; the lost man, plantation.* Or maybe it was the other way around.

In any case they certainly were opposites, she thought, while the terrain grew darker and the foliage thicker. As Mann's property was distanced further with every step, so was Joy psychically transported from him and his needs. Her prophecy was received and now there was little to impart; he was largely on his own until the one's arrival. He was called to prepare for the life fate had pledged to him, whereas she was summoned to dispense with the symbol of death sadly wallowing in the distance. The man and his counsel were always, and by definition, inhabiting extremes of conscious existence, but in this moment the contrast was as stark as ever.

The solitude of the forest enabled Joy to recall some of her life before Mann. The memories came to her in images tied by mysterious associations to her environs. There was something in the way the sunlight winnowed through the leaves and branches that cast her mind upon a memory of her own seclusion many years ago. She was gripped by *déjà vu*. It was not the same forest but one quite the same in appearance, and she had the same feeling of dread without fear.

She had her own counsel once. He was a very old man of an exceptionally serious demeanor. From the moment she met him it seemed to her that his innocence was once not merely lost but mercilessly crushed. He treated her with kindness as best he could, but the sadness of his soul overwhelmed all other sentiments in him. Though he was her counsel, she wished for his happiness often, and suspected that his mind was tortured by an unspeakable pain.

Nevertheless, he mastered his obligation, took parental care of her and made her consummately ready for her one. His prophecy was perfect. He described her one in exact detail and was elaborate and precise in instructing her preparations to receive him. Her counsel had a majestic way with words, a talent remaining from an aged generation that she admired and swore to preserve and impart upon whoever would come into her care. When her counsel spoke, he conjured images. There was always something said and something meant, a simultaneity of complex proportions that unified truth and morals.

Her one was, in no uncertain terms, regal. He exuded grace and benevolence with a commanding presence, traits she perceived the moment she first saw him. It was love at first sight in a way, although she loved him well before meeting. He loved her deeply, too. Their convergence felt less like an introduction than a reunion, or more like a pardon to consummate a forbidden love. Their courtship began in such a manner and continued that way, every day, until the end.

Joy knew why she remembered this. Her memory was a deep emotional burden that filled her heart with regret. By now she was well into the valley. The swell of another hill lay before her, and her foreboding intuition directed her forward. She missed her one now perhaps more than ever.

David A. Colón

The time she had with him in many ways taught her everything she knew about love and fate, as brief as it was relative to the span of her entire life. There was no substitute for his company, and nothing could duplicate the sensation of thrill and comfort that touching him afforded. Every word he spoke vibrated like a note of music, every glance he aimed landed like a thrust, and when he shared with her the depths to which his hopes entwined with hers, she thanked her fate in worshipping tones.

The recollection seemed equally distant and recent. She felt lonely for lack of that loving embrace yet could imagine it so completely. Now she walked—it seemed as if she was afoot ever since. Life was a continuous journey, sympathy the only thing wavering.

The hill steepened, and she ascended it like a staircase.

Instantly, her sentiment was evacuated, her mind possessed by the force of prevision. She knew she was near; a montage of moments into the future invaded her perception of the present. Awareness skipped along the fabric of reality, pausing her experience of the continuum of time. She saw a dark form, an indistinguishable person, lying in a brush but a minute or two away. The shade of light of the image was slightly brighter than the space she was in now, the leap from future to present providing the points of action she needed to connect.

Calm though her mind was, the pace of her beating heart quickened. Two paths of thought interwove and intensified the circumstances. The memory of her one returned, the rueful time when he confided fear to her and she in turn learned of her true fate. If not still held by obedience, she would have allowed resentment to overcome her, but in that moment of youth she lacked the fortitude to challenge the dominion of destiny. She complied with fortune, then as she did now. But the timbre of satanic contest echoed faintly in her heart

The Lost Men

forever.

*   *

She took a step, and there he was. The mass she foresaw moments earlier was now with her: past, present, future, braided into one. A lost man was to be pursued with caution, even—and, really, only—when in mortal throes. She knew it was he. She fixed her gaze upon him and circled as silently as she could. He did not move but was still alive. As she approached she could see him respire, his chest heaving in short, quick pants.

He rested prone before her, spread on the earth like an inverted crucifix. He was dressed in black, and still faceless, and propped up a bit by the rucksack still strapped beneath his body. His hair was a wild, filthy mane of streaked locks, and now she could hear his weakening gasps. He reeked of death: his own and a hundred others. The questions she had could hardly be contained:

Why is he compelled to kill? How many lives had he dispatched? What manner of man is he? Was he not raised by parents? Was he not mentored by a counsel? Did he ever love? Did he choose to hate? Could he feel? Does he hope? Does fate address him? Had he ever doubted? Does he repent? Can he speak? How was he ever born? Why was he ever born?

She stood in silence, seized by curiosity. Above all else she wanted to know if, in far greater terms, he was a cause or a symptom. No one knew why history had taken the path mankind weathered in this age of attrition. Every soul left reflected on this question yet had no recourse to the truth. There were myriad signs but only rendered through speculation, all empty of meaning, phenomena without noumena. To say that lost men were the agents of

David A. Colón

man's demise was akin to claiming rain fell to grow flowers.

Though it was certain that he had killed more people than he could remember. He was the living embodiment of a mass grave, his flesh the fossilized sediment of every soul he disgraced. With each murder he grew more adept at killing, a skill he cultivated the way others practiced music or pottery. He had butchered, strangled, burned, and defenestrated; suffocated, decapitated, bludgeoned, even scared to death. He worked tirelessly to kill, the way one like Mann labored religiously to gain knowledge and foster talents. While Mann toiled to preserve abilities and history, the lost man fought against this tide of hope with equally determined efficiency. The two manifested the dialectical extremes of the evanescent human condition, and as much as it was impossible to know the reason why, so was it unsure which force was justified.

But the sins of humankind seemed archaic in the present. It must have been a dozen years since the lost man had encountered another person, for so few remained. The lost man was, in effect, obsolete—if ever there was a duty he served. If lost men were meant to purge mankind of its waste and profanity, that was certainly achieved. If it was not, then the charge of lost men could only have been to erase humanity altogether, and at this point, with no further assistance, odds were overwhelmingly in favor of this morbid fruition. Any alternative explanation of lost men would be incomprehensible. The parallel struggles of killers and those who beget life could only be understood as antithetical. But as Joy stood over the dying man, her repulsion seeped into a kind of ambivalence. He was damned; his actions complied; she felt remorse. Counsels were meant to see and feel, especially predicaments like this.

And then the lost man moved. He slowly, very slowly,

The Lost Men

tilted his head back, his face finally coming into view. It moved as if he was already aware of her presence. He stopped with his head hanging backwards, his face upside down.

When he laid eyes upon her, their gazes locked. His eyes were a twilight gray, and even in this inverted position she could see the danger in him. He was very old and bearded, as her counsel once was, but there was nothing taciturn about this man. Wisdom did not accumulate in the lost man. Age pulled the skin without pushing the mind.

Without a moment to think, his shoulder tensed, visibly through his clothes, but his arm barely moved. In his hand he held a Kalashnikov and tried to point it at her but it would not rise from the ground. Joy watched in patient amazement. His finger pulled the trigger and the rifle clicked. A second passed and his tightened shoulder softened. Her eyes returned from his arm to his face, and she could tell that he was dead.

*   *

None of the lost man's possessions were of personal worth. Joy sorted through his belongings and found no photographs, no memorabilia, no written notes or heirlooms. His rucksack was filled with worn camping supplies and a cache of ammunition for his two firearms. Nothing with him or about him identified him as a unique person. He did not even keep trophies of his victims.

She stripped him bare. His dull yellow body was bony and sickly, a raisin of the once dense and strong frame he had long ago. The hands and feet were thickened, from overuse and scar tissue; his passage from this world left behind a casing of exhaustion. Weathered by struggle, the corpse had been wrung of its last drop of life, and Joy was

David A. Colón

reminded of Sisyphus, if he were to have been alleviated of his eternal punishment.

She grabbed his clothing, equipment, and weapons and carried them to the heap of timber she piled nearby. Two long, sturdy spits stood on either side of the kindling and she spread the items in the middle of the woodpile.

The memories returned. They were wrought with sadness, an uncontrollable grief unlike the coolness of the present. At that time long ago, though anguished, she struggled to not weep as she scavenged fallen branches and hacked tree limbs with her axe. She selected the thickest and straightest boughs and erected the finest pyre that she could. Each pole sounded a hollow knock when laid across the spits, details that, one by one, deepened the feeling of finality. Mustering what sensed like her last ounce of strength, she lifted the body into her arms—then, the body of her one; now, the body of the lost man. She laid the men onto their wooden beds, folded their hands on their chests, doused the branches with kerosene, and paused. And suddenly, with the toss of a lit match, the pyres erupted into eager flames. The fire sailed upward against the pale sky: then, she wept; now, she sighed. For hours she fed the blaze with kindling, well through the night, the forms rendered delicate ashes. *Tomorrow will provide a new course of duties.* In the present, she had to counsel Mann's expectancy; in the memory, she knew she was to receive prevision. Her mind unsealed and truths poured in. The smoke smelled like vengeance. Like an echo. Like Echo.

Four

The next morning the house smelled like ashes from the roast. Its white walls were bright with the newness of day. Windows let in rays of sun, contrasting the shadowy fireplace. The air of the room was still although outside there was activity.

Faith packed busily for the journey. Though Paine advised her to rest that night, she found it almost impossible to sleep. News of the one came as a great comfort, but a fleeting sense of safety: soon washed away by the rip tide of unexpected work to be done.

In the moment of hearing the prophecy, Faith felt regal, almost holy. Through the mouthpiece of her counsel, fate spoke to her, no one else: it felt as if it had one voice, one tongue and one pair of lips, addressing in that very moment her and only her. Halted by the attention, she sensed the roles of power inverted. Fate was not master but servant, asking for *her* to command and be merciful, begging for *her* to conduct the business of order, praying for *her* to merit such allegiance.

But she remembered Paine's advice and knew to be humble. She slept a few hours that night and in the morning her thoughts had matured. It became clear that her sole purpose now was to seek out the one, and ideas of him began to surface. *He, too, must be wrestling with the same issues—or quite possibly different ones.* She quickly grew to respect his sentience, for now he was no longer a myth but real.

* *

Having wandered alongside the shore, Paine came to rest in a clearing at the edge of a cliff. On a large stone he sat and viewed the giant stillness of the lake. In the furthest distance a small white boat lay in the water tied to a dark wooden dock. It appeared motionless, as did the rest of the scene, the kind of frozen image invariably cast on any eye. Empty of civilization, the world was everywhere a tranquil landscape, a placid portrait that mirrored patience to even the fiercest gaze.

The lake was a reservoir. Dappled with tiny, silent waves, the expanse of the water reminded Paine of the ocean, the root of a hundred memories. There was no smell of salty brine in the air, no crash of breakers aged a thousand leagues, but the awesome force of indomitable presence was the same. The sea was another world within this one, a sovereign realm that land was content to respect and ignore and at times necessarily fear.

The recollections were of varied origins, just as the fears were due to both nature and man. *How terrified the people of this continent must have been to witness the first European galleons emerge from the fog.* From his earliest memories as a boy, Paine was fascinated by tales of conquest. The legendary history immortalizing the clashes of civilizations was his childhood obsession. Paine was an astute boy, and the signs he displayed of his intellectual abilities encouraged his parents to grant him some autonomy in pursuing his early studies. Equally temperamental, Paine frowned upon mathematics, science, and trades. He spent all the time he could reading history and historical literature, anything martial in particular.

David A. Colón

Growing into his determined specialty, the philosophical, ethical, and compassionate appendages of his mind, it could be said, withered. It took great pains to resuscitate these faculties when called upon to counsel.

He remembered a conversation he had long ago. He was barely nine years old, and rapt in recounting one of his readings over lunch.

"Mama," he asked, "what is a pilgrimage?"

Warmed by her son's precociousness, she answered happily, "A pilgrimage was a journey one took to a sacred place, or, in a looser sense, a search for spiritual understanding or enlightenment."

The boy considered each word she spoke, one by one. After the pause, he said, "I read some of the *Canterbury Tales* today."

"You did?"

"Yes I did."

"Which ones did you read?"

"Hold on, wait," he said. "I still don't understand what a pilgrimage is."

His mother replied, "Tell me what you don't understand about it."

The boy spoke quickly, "I don't get what you mean by a sacred place, or spiritual, or…*intellement*."

Privy to the proper context—the book—she said, "Hmm. A long time ago, when there were many people..."

"I know *that*," the boy interrupted.

"When there were many people," she patiently resumed, "there was a time when most of them believed in God." The boy had been adequately schooled in the concept and various scriptures, so no explanation of God was needed. "And some believed that there were certain places where God's influence was stronger than in the rest of the world. Usually these places were churches, or cathedrals, or monasteries"—she enunciated the words deliberately to jar the boy's recall of terms she had taken efforts to teach to him in lessons—"or temples, places where people came together to worship God and conduct ceremonies." She paused for a moment. "Some of these places were also known for things that happened in them, like if a great person was born there, or if a king and a queen were married there, or if a beloved person died there..."

"Like St. Thomas à Becket, who was killed in Canterbury Cathedral," the boy declared confidently.

"That's right," the mother said. She thought that next her son would ask why Becket was killed, but he did not.

"So why would someone do a pilgrimage?"

"Someone would *make* a pilgrimage to one of these places to honor the memory of what happened there or honor the memory of a person connected to that place. People believed that it pleased God to do that, and also that making a pilgrimage made them better people because they thought it was good to show respect to people they thought were honest and decent and righteous." She answered all the questions that she could. "So which tales did you read?"

He picked up the book from under the table. It was a small red paperback with a picture of a colorful painting on the cover. "I read the Prologue and I read the Franklin's Tale."

"Oh," the mother said, "you skipped to the Franklin's Tale?"

"Yes."

"Why?"

He shrugged. "I don't know," he said in a questioning tone.

"You read about the Franklin in the Prologue and you thought he was the most interesting?"

"Mm hmm," he replied.

"So why'd you like him so much?"

David A. Colón

"Because he eats a lot of good food and has a big house like us."

His mother chuckled. "That's true," she answered happily. "But I thought you'd like the Knight more."

"I like him, too. I'll read his tale next. But the Franklin's Tale's about a knight, too."

"Oh yes?"

"Yes, and he sails far away to fight in a war and is gone for two years," he said with zeal.

"Well what happens in the tale?" his mother asked.

"First the knight falls in love with a lady, and she becomes his one. And they love each other and are very good to each other. And then the knight has to sail away to go to war and leaves her alone, and she gets very sad. And she has lots of friends and they try to make her happy but she can't stop feeling sad. And the knight is gone for a long time and then the lady meets another man who says he loves her, too, but when he tells her that he loves her she tells him that she would never love him because she loves the knight. But she makes a mistake and jokes with the other man and says that she would love him, too, if he could make all the rocks by the beach disappear. So the man goes to a magician and offers him money to make the rocks disappear, but when the man is gone to see the magician, the knight comes back and the lady is happy. But in the meantime the magician does it and then the man goes back to the woman and shows her the beach and all the rocks are gone and then she gets sad again because she said that she'd love him if he could do that, and she doesn't want to be a liar. But she loves her one and so she tells her one what happened and he says that he would never want her to be someone who doesn't keep her promises and so he says it's okay and that she should leave him and take the other man to be her one. So she tells the other man that she'll do it but then *he* gets sad because he

The Lost Men

thinks that it's not right to do that to her and the knight and so he gives up and goes back to the magician to pay him the money he promised to pay him, but he doesn't have all the money and so he asks the magician if he can pay him back later and the magician asks why and so the man tells the magician what happened and the magician says that it's okay and that he doesn't have to pay him the rest of the money."

She was delighted by her son's story. "Wonderful. And that's how the tale ends?"

"Yes," said the boy, his cheeks a little flushed.

His mother leaned forward. "So what do you think this means?"

"I don't know," he singsonged.

"Well, don't you think everyone acted kindly in the end?"

The boy nodded.

"And don't you think that honesty and forgiveness triumphed over selfish desire?"

He nodded again, this time smiling, as if she put into words ideas already in his head.

"Very good, Paine. Remember that—you should always pursue that which you want, but when you see a better path, then you should choose it."

The boy hung his head, the look one makes when schooled of ethics. But his thoughts were already elsewhere. "Mama," he said, "I wonder what it's like to sail far away."

She was taken aback by the sudden redirection. "Why?"

"The knight goes away for so long. If he didn't go away, the whole story wouldn't have happened."

"That's true."

"And why was it that whenever people sailed far away they fought a war?"

She shook her head with concern. "That's not always

David A. Colón

true."

"Yes it is," he retorted. "Everything I've read about sailing in ships to faraway lands means there's war." He spoke with conviction; the sea had become a metonym for violence. And the truth was it held for him more allure than repugnance.

She thought for a moment, recalling books he had read and the books she had read, and there was something to it; he had a point, and she was dismayed. Perhaps it was the nature of historical record, perhaps yet another one of the great character flaws of the world of population, but either idea was too difficult to explain adequately to the boy.

Words came faster to him than to her, and so he continued to speak. "I wish I could be a soldier and sail away and fight..." He imagined holding a sword in his fists, wearing armor and slashing his way through swarms of faceless men. Having never met any people, he envisioned them all as if wild animals, slaughtering them the way he did toads and beetles. Imposing deadly will on living things was a way for him to assert his independence and validate his power, an urge that had been welling gradually in him as he approached puberty.

His mother wisely knew that admonition was moot and that the best way to sway him from this fantasy was gently. "It's best not to think of the sea as a road to battle," she said. "That's not the true motive of seafaring travelers. I agree with you that history has often painted that picture, but that is only part of the story." She paused to get his attention. "When groups of people took to sea, even when they were armies, it was never with the *pure* intention to fight. Maritime explorations were always for relief, to relieve the societies from whence they came of overpopulation, or famine, or meager opportunities." She tried as best she could to stay on the side of euphemism, but it was not even a half-truth. For the sake of her son's future, this lie needed to be told. "I'm not saying war never existed, of course it did: but violence was never an end in itself. Many wars were fought in an attempt to bring hope to people, to find a new home, to start a new society, to begin a new culture." The more she spoke, the more she tasted deceit. In mentoring her son, she processed various strategies instantaneously and abandoned the ruse. "Some day, when you're older, you'll read the *Aeneid* and see exactly what I mean. As much as the *Aeneid* glorifies war—and believe me, it does—one cannot lose sight of its most important lesson: we, people, are destined to survive, to establish homes and our lives and ensure the continuance of humanity even in the face of cruelty and misfortune."

*   *

Paine eventually did read the poem. It was nine years later, when he was eighteen and preparing himself to accept his parents leaving him on his own. He had reached maturity, meaning it was time for him to enter his solitude, and he came to terms with his parents' embarkation in part by studying the exile of Aeneas. In the *Aeneid*, the chorus of gods and spirits echoed fate's will, and the impact of this device strengthened his faith in the power and benevolence of destiny. No longer was military fantasy his fetish; he was a young man, and the responsibility of perseverance had taken root. Over the years, duty, like a steady trickle of water, gave contour to the bedrock of his mind, and without any discussion he knew to protect his mother's lies, to bury the intentions of the crime of war. The sea had transformed in his thoughts, from an altar for death to a symbol of transience, but transience was not a source of inspiration the way legends of heroes were. He was ambivalent about his parents leaving, for he knew it

David A. Colón

was their fate and time for him to live as a man yet it was sorrowful to say goodbye to the only people he had ever known. They defined life, his sun and moon. *Perhaps their journey would take them by sea*, but he could not bear to contemplate their future very long. It brought him pain, could drive him mad, for their departure signaled his induction into adulthood, the true purpose in life and the only hope for the future. The world was to be his and he was to be Atlas, sorrow ringing in his mind like the wail of sirens, and he knew better than to torment himself with suffering for curiosity, since of this ship he was both captain and crew.

*   *

Nine years later he was summoned to receive his one. He had been with his counsel for merely three years before the advent.

"The one will come by sea," the woman told him. "She has already embarked on her journey, and has been traversing the ocean for weeks now."

For weeks at sea. Paine's interest in the ocean was rekindled in but a moment. He was weary of his world; the routine of chores in his mundane life was suffocating him, and he longed to flee. He thought about taking to the water, like his one, and passing over thousands of miles, adrift at the mercy of wave and wind, day after night after day in the wild expanse of ocean and its mean uniformity. *Sailing between continents must be like crawling on the skin of the earth*, its largest organ, pulsing and alive and purposeful and yet mindless. The sea was a reminder of man's stature: a forgettable speck. Paine wanted to lose himself that way, to taste the permanence of death while alive. He was jealous of his one.

He was seized by fantasy as his counsel instructed him

The Lost Men

of the preparations. She spoke but the force of his own thoughts barricaded his mind. He barely retained her instructions—to revive the lighthouse, to sew new clothes, to serve no meat at the feast.

He had finished sewing his ensemble, an embroidered suit of black silk in an Asian style, and was dressed for the occasion. When it was time he walked to the beach alone. His counsel watched from a balcony window as the vessel slowed to the dock. The ship dropped anchor and the memory of that conversation with his mother returned. Paine was standing on a flattened jetty of boulders, like the ones Aurelius made vanish for Dorigen, and he finally agreed that, yes, faring the sea could bring new life and hope.

Counsel in tow, she introduced herself as Charity. Their meeting was cold and, though polite, noticeably charged with pretense. He took her hand and walked her to his home. She said little, and he said nothing.

*   *

Paine retracted from the memory and his senses returned. He had been staring at the lake as Faith prepared for their departure, and though the memories vanished, their feeling lingered like a vivid dream. Not a day in his life passed without remembering his one, and likewise every remembrance ended as abruptly. And, likewise, afterwards he always felt hatred for himself.

He stood and walked from the clearing back to the path he took from the house. He did not look back but hastened away, almost as if he had pushed himself off that hidden cliff. It was no matter that he would never see this lake again. There were glorious views everywhere, and reminiscence persistently managed to sicken them.

His fleeting steps were a remedy. Faith's journey was

the matter at hand, and the speed of dutiful pace made him feel worthy to live. His mind was caked with confusion, teetering on an emotional crest. The name *Charity* whispered repeatedly in his head, in her voice and in his. The utterances became syncopated, bombarding him with torment, and he quickened to the clumsy gallop of one trying to elude his own shadow. The gluttonous image of the banquet table appeared, with its platters of half-eaten food shifted carelessly. Suppressed feelings were awakening and he was panicked. But he was accustomed to this struggle and this time, like every other time, he would overcome it. The means were always different but the cunning was a practiced skill.

He reached the lawn behind the house. It was a cause for serenity. Faith appeared inadvertently: loading the last of their belongings into the vehicle. Her form was like an angel to him, a giver of hope and grace. Her concentration on her tasks and oblivion to his plight were a relief. She radiated innocence.

"There you are," she said happily, and a little out of breath. "I was wondering when you'd get back."

"I'm sorry," he said.

"Oh, not at all." She moved busily, opening and closing doors to the vehicle. She slammed the last, sighed deeply, and stood before him. With arms akimbo and a beaming smile, she asked:

"Are you hungry?"

The question made him dizzy. His mouth watered. The images returned, as did the shame. He was standing, holding a knife, his hands warm and slick with blood. Charity was dead. It was unspeakable. *Contra naturam.* The work of a Wendigo.

But fate was subject to no taboo. He merely obeyed.

"No," he replied. "But *you* should definitely eat something before we go."

Five

Faith and Paine rode in the vehicle, with the windows rolled down, on a wide highway. The metallic hum of the engine, the gentle scraping of the spinning wheels, the faint rattle of the trailer in tow, the rustle of wind surging through the cabin: a symphony. Each swell of the roadway led to a temporary vista before a gradual descent, and at the top, in the span of a blink, the two could see twenty miles ahead. The highway was straight, parting once-fertile land now empty as far as the eye could see. The deep blue sky was like a dome, making the endless space feel contained and, in a sense, constricting. Large green and white metal signs marked the names of exits and streets, and every dozen miles a sign depicting a blue and red shield appeared by the roadside.

Faith felt happy, and Paine felt sad. His experiences stained the moment with fear, repeatedly clenched by paralysis, the minutes passing like a million split-second lifetimes. She, on the other hand, could hardly maintain her composure. An elation she had never felt coursed through her body.

"Have you received any clearer visions of him?" she asked, breaking the hour-long silence.

Paine flinched. She rescued him from his thoughts, and for this he obliged. "Yes I have."

The truth was he had not. He knew she was

The Lost Men

overwhelmed with eagerness and curiosity and so, out of tenderness, he decided to reconstitute visions he had seen before of the one into new, more elaborate, more nuanced descriptions. Being a counsel meant you could never lie.

"*So?*" she blurted, eyebrows raised, baring her teeth in a genuine grin.

He feigned a smile.

She failed to notice it was fake.

"Well what do you want to know?"

"*Hhhhh*," she groaned with comic exasperation. "What's he like? What's his strong suit? What am I to expect when I meet him? Come *on*, Paine!"

"Okay, okay," he replied, smiling, looking down. "He has many virtues."

"Good."

"He is capable and resourceful, and has a magnificent home. You should find it exquisite, if not luxurious."

"*Goooood*," she said, her voice tailing up for motivation.

He moved along as she clearly wished. "He is also very talented, and his talents are divers. He is an extraordinary cook—the banquet should be *divine*."

"I can't wait," she said, with a daydreaming look in her eyes.

"He is a talented musician as well. Since his childhood he has practiced several instruments and has eclectic tastes." He envisioned a private concert, then realized it was most likely. "He will play for us once we're there—maybe even at the banquet. Actually, yes, he will play for us at the banquet." This guarantee was a safe bet, and gambling with a prediction like this made Paine more excited and enthused. If the one did *not* play music for them at the feast, well, then, he could claim fate changed its mind.

"He is also a painter," he added. "He has studied fine art in books and has notable ability." He paused. "Maybe he will paint a portrait of you."

"Of *me?*" she asked in mock humility. Everything she said tottered on the brink of laughter.

"Of course of you," he responded. "You'd be his most cherished subject." He flirted with getting carried away. "In fact, I'm certain of it."

Faith blushed. She was sure he was right and too gleeful to remember what she said angrily, two days before, about there being no artists left in the world. "But what about *him?* What's his personality like?"

Paine thought for a moment. "I told you before of his magnificent home, and you should consider it an outward manifestation of his character. It is awe-inspiring and profound, like him. It has many rooms and chambers, many assets of wide-ranging use. It is full of books and art and elegance and devotion, and he is just the same."

She listened attentively. Her smile was replaced with an expression of inspiration, the kind of look one gives when proud of a stranger.

"He is exacting," Paine continued. "The first sign you'll see of this will be his carefully manicured grounds. He doesn't overuse land, mining just what he needs to ensure security, and takes remarkable care of that which he controls. I think he will be the same way with you." This noticeably pleased Faith; she wanted to keep the discussion on topic, meaning the impact of all of this on her.

"This should make him a good and trustworthy partner, but he will also be a good companion. I have no sense that he is as jovial as *you* are," he said with a nod to Faith, who acknowledged him with a charming glance, "but he is good-humored. He has wit, and grace, and an ability to disarm any person with a clever remark or an unpretentious saying. I think you'll be thrilled to know him."

"Of course, of course—I'm so happy to hear everything you say, Paine. I don't think you realize just how much I've dreamed of him."

"Oh, I think I do," he responded.

But dreaming meant different things to the two. She longed for the future, he longed for a second chance; she expected, he regretted. It was cruel that despair knew of hope, but that hope never learned the lessons of despair: that it was intrinsic to experience that suffering needed to have felt ecstasy in order to exist, and not the other way around.

"I've dreamed of him so much," she confided, "that I hope I haven't set my expectations of him too high."

"Nonsense," Paine said, still pacifying. "He will be everything you've hoped for. His ethics are firmly grounded, and he is a potent intellect."

She remembered this last quality; it was the first Paine ever imparted to her. He had been receiving sporadic visions of the one for several years, but the very first he had was of a man with a keen mind. For this reason Faith had spent much of her adult life reading and learning, forcing herself to retain specifics in support of conjecture and studying every experience as a text. One of her favorite maxims, one she readily recalled whenever reflecting on her condition and which had become a mantra of sorts, came from *Rasselas*: "Long journeys in search of truth are not commanded. Truth, such as is necessary to the regulation of life, is always found where it is honestly sought."

This tenet defined her intellectual life, but now her mind was forced into such a long journey—though the search was not for truth, but love. To quest for love was equally a departure and a return: a break with the past and an entrance to the beyond. It meant leaving behind what she knew of herself in order to discover an emotional home that had always resided within her. And knowing that her one was a man of intelligence and learning, the mysteries of hope she regarded through erudition and metaphor. It was important not only to come to terms with her experiences but also to communicate them meaningfully to her one: to explain her trials as Odyssean, to summate her urges as Daedalean.

But reflecting on life, not words, came more naturally to her. She knew as much and hoped this patent difference between herself and her one, if it were fate to expose it, would not breed conflict in their companionship but rather complement one another. It was in his nature to read, in her nature to explore, two very distinct mindsets and outlooks on experience. She did the best she could to fashion herself into a fit match, and—just as she had with augmenting her modes of survival—she envisioned myriad possibilities of this impending union. However, it was largely guesswork, for Paine could not confidently predict the outcome of their marriage.

She referred to her parents. In her memory of them they were essentially opposites, but it worked quite well. Their personalities were polar extremes: night and day, calm and storm, bee and blossom: and like these tandems they would have had no existence without each other, were in fact defined and fed and relieved by the ones they were not. Her father was quiet and reserved, literal and practical, a man who seemed to calculate, every second of his life, the exact amount of energy necessary to complete the task at hand and then expend it without wasting even the most negligible surplus—including his affections for his daughter, in which he knew that generosity was appropriate, but she was never spoiled or smothered.

And while her father minded his resources like a banker, her mother cast hers about like a gambler. She was a woman of verve, ebullient and loud and animated and forever happy, whose will could not be dampened by the grimmest specter or deepest tragedy. The firm division between their temperaments was fixed in Faith's mind, and the memories she had of her upbringing were equally compartmentalized. Her mother took her hunting, read to her, went on hikes with her, sharing and teaching everything subject to imprecision, patience, or poetry. Contrarily, her father schooled her in botany and gardening, game playing, plumbing, and hygiene, all species of anatomy of one form or another. She felt lucky to have had such diverse parents, rich in difference and humanity, and remembered the glee of once being a family: how her father would sometimes laugh, how her mother always rested assured.

*   *

The green and white exit signs became more common—Faith slowed to drive around one that had fallen, bent and twisted, in the middle of the highway. They sped under an overpass when a faint urban mirage appeared on the horizon.

"Is that Omaha?" Faith asked.

"I think so," Paine responded.

The sight of the city made her drive faster. Within minutes they were close enough to see the details of the buildings: the windows, the bricks. Faith had turned right onto Route 6, which passed through the center of Council Bluffs. When they saw the welcome sign to the city, Faith thought for a moment and said, "Council Bluffs, huh? So did they name the city after the lies you tell me?"

Paine's expression remained the same, but Faith chuckled to herself.

The desolate city felt hollow, a scaffold erected around a quiet melancholy. The somberness was not of a paradise lost but of a void of any such possibility ever. It felt like a place where man should never have lived and yet there were monuments nonetheless. Dry, rusted fountains and cement troughs where flowers once grew in abundance moated the halls of Commerce and Justice. The vehicle allowed the two to tour the town with haste, a three-minute montage of an architectural echo.

The road ended at a river. "This is the Missouri," Paine announced. What was left of the Douglas Street Bridge lay before them, two nubs on either side of the water. The middle of the bridge was gone; the scars where the center severed off were neat.

She asked, "Do you know if there's another way across?"

"I'm sure there is," he replied. "Let's follow the river north."

She shifted into reverse, backed the vehicle and its trailer into a turn and retraced their path until veering off onto the exit "29N." For several miles the road curved along the east bank of the river. In a short while they were faced by a winding complex of intersecting freeways.

"We'll try here," Faith declared. She drove through the maze and headed west, and saw the crossing. "Oh, *how beautiful*."

There were two bridges, identical twins. Four massive concrete columns, embedded in the water, supported two viaducts caged in crisscrossed metal bars. The steel was painted lime green, an homage to oxidation.

"This is the Mormon Bridge," Paine stated.

Faith looked at him. "Which one?"

"Both of them. That's the Old Mormon Bridge, and that's the New Mormon Bridge."

"Well, they look the same to me." A moment passed. "That's really what they're called? This is the *Mormon* Bridge?"

The Lost Men

"Yes."

She was smitten by the omen. The previous day she was studying the Book of Mormon when Paine provided his prophecy. The train of thought vanished upon his announcement, but now it returned: the promise of benevolence, the conviction that devotion is inherently good, the premise of a lost testament of the canon of scripture that will save humanity from its denial of the true moral responsibility—her determination was fueled by the allegory.

"I think it's safe," Paine said.

"So do I."

They closed the doors and slowly drove over the bridge to the right. They could feel the river beneath them, its gentle flow and constancy like the harmless heaves of a sleeping elephant. The roadway of the bridge spilled onto land, leading them around the north side of Omaha. Faith had never visited this city before and felt regretful for not taking the opportunity to explore it further. The journey ahead was long, and to complete it in the three days Paine foresaw would require discipline and constant motion.

The road bent south and passed through the western edge of the metropolis. After crossing several thoroughfares, Faith felt a bit anxious. "We're going due south and we need to get west," she blurted desperately. Then, more calmly, she said, "I'm taking this." She turned right onto a road that soon was labeled "92W." And in minutes the city was gone.

*   *

The terrain grew barren again, more ruined farmland left to its own nature. Like a domesticated animal set free in the wild, the earth stood little chance to survive once abandoned by its caretakers. It was a dangerous place for

David A. Colón

Faith and Paine to be in, for there were no resources whatsoever. This was a motivating force of their expedition.

Soon they passed another river, much smaller, and continued due west. After several more minutes of growing consternation, the roadway ended in an offering of two opposite directions.

"I thought this would have connected with 80 by now," Faith said.

Paine was at a loss, looked around, and said nothing.

To the left the road was crooked; to the right, perfectly straight. Without hesitation, Faith turned north onto the linear path. "If this doesn't get us there soon, we'll turn around."

*   *

The vehicle slowed almost to a stop. On the side of the road was a small–billboard, and what was left of its swooping script read, "Welcome to C—."

Beyond the billboard, the scene was surreal; the town had been razed to smithereens, a desert of driftwood, flat as the sea and a thousand miles inland with subtle swells, some more of brick and others of plywood, and most of indistinguishable material. It appeared that over the centuries C— had been pounded by tornadoes, the winds reshredding the same heap of cedar and glass until blended into a coarse silt.

The flatness of it all was most striking. Relative to the sprawl of the plain, C— was sprinkled about like an accident. Faith stopped the vehicle at the lip of the debris, and she and her counsel got out for a closer look.

It was remarkable how small C— was; a mere handful of acres contained the entire place. Faith began to tread the impasto of wood chips and crumbled cement, and even her

The Lost Men

lonesome eyes could not deny the evidence that this had to be the littlest society the world of population had ever known. Beneath the four-inch crust of flakes and splinters was a grid of eight intersecting streets. The fact that she could see the beginning and end of each one from a single, central vantage felt, in an unfamiliar way, appalling. The trait of the gone world that she appreciated most was its record of achievement, but C— was, in no uncertain terms, petty and unambitious.

She imagined why, and the truth revealed itself. She walked through C— with her eyes to the ground, spotting rusty bolts and screws, noting that only a culture ideologically committed to self-repression could cauterize its natural growth so dramatically. She had no inkling that beneath her feet lay the foundation of the former St. Joseph's Catholic Church, and she felt that a patent contentment with mediocrity was the kind of sin only an overcrowded world could commit.

The nostalgia that found quaint such a town died with the people. She thought a culture that valued social insulation had to be, by definition, unwelcoming, and at this moment Faith failed to realize that even in the world of population there were shelters from human traffic. Nevertheless, she was right about the ethos of C—, for it had been grateful for its isolation in the most mendacious of ways. At the core of C—'s inhabitants, undiluted for generations, was a curious pride in accepting harsh fate. Winters killed children before vaccination and scant crop yields inflicted slow deaths upon fathers, but the words of the men in black with white collars were strong and unforgiving, and C— comforted in ignorance.

Faith stopped walking to register an observation; she was amazed at how fine were the bits beneath her feet. As extensive as the damage was, and with nothing to collide with but itself, C— must have weathered the wrath of

David A. Colón

dozens of cyclones. She bent down to scoop a handful of the shards and noticed the fragments were soft and rounded. The dust felt almost pitiful, a sign of the extent to which C— was powerless to external forces: these of nature, but perhaps of man as well. Such a tiny place so remotely tucked could have no real perspective on the world, on what it and its people were truly capable of in all of life's various circumstances.

C— was built around the church, two grain silos and a post office, and for four generations it stayed that way. People spoke slowly, were scared of the unfamiliar: were intolerant, overly judicial, obedient to shallow demands. *Pride* was a word they used often as camouflage: a gesture-turned-reflex, a talisman for their vacancy. Faith pitched pebbles and felt strongly. *These people, for any reason—but none enough to absolve them—did not grasp the charge of humanity. There is always more to life than survival, diversion, and worship.*

She circled around the center of C— and Paine came into view. He was standing, one hand holding the other wrist behind his back, before a narrow, rusted pedestal sprouting from the debris. At its top, about waist high, it was missing the oak and Plexiglas case that had long ago presented readers with a history of a landmark. The pole stood like a persistent weed whose head of spores had blown away. But this feeble token, even if the two would have been privy to its purpose, was not penance enough. It was as much for C—'s inattentiveness to posterity as for the doings of natural decay and calamity that there was no recourse to history or origins. Without a commitment to understanding and realizing the greatest good mankind could achieve, there was no awareness then, hence any memory now.

The woman and her counsel looked at each other and in silence returned to their vehicle. Faith could not believe that C— could have existed in the former world she had studied and imagined. But the sad truth was that C—, Nebraska was as real a place as there had ever been.

*   *

She could sense the cruelty ebb in her mind without the onset of guilt. Paine sat still as she drove down the highway, heading west again, again in search of their lost way. The thoughts of the wrecked scene left a fetid residue in her mind. She kept telling herself that ignorance was no excuse; to not know that the future would dispatch civilization's lifeblood was beside the point. No one ever knew the future in its entirety: not even counsels; not the politicians, who failed to protect their citizens from the purges; not priests and not mothers; not artists and not scientists; and yet this had no bearing on living with conviction and great responsibility, siring the kinds of achievements that reveal truths and bear fruits of knowledge that evolve life closer and closer to the divine. Comparing her own life to the lives people once lived, she felt licensed to pass this judgment.

Soon enough the image faded away. She wiped tears from her cheeks without Paine noticing, as she had many times before.

"Do you think this is the right path?" Paine asked without glancing from the road ahead.

"I don't know," she answered in a barely wavering tone. She cleared her throat and sobered up. "But I need a break. I'm hungry. D'you think if we find somewhere we can settle in that we can eat and stock fuel?"

Paine said yes, grateful that she was the one who suggested it.

In a few miles, and hoping Paine's hunch was right, Faith turned north onto Route 15. The road was clean.

David A. Colón

Hardly any time passed before the town came into view, and the first sign of it was living plant life. As dramatic as a mountain's tree line, the green of grasses and bush presented itself at the entrance to the town. After so much desolation through the lifeless steppe of the heartland, to the outsiders it was a miracle that the town appeared so bright and confident.

On the right was an airport consisting of a modest hangar and landing strip. Faith momentarily imagined flying to her one, a euphoric fantasy, and then something occurred to her.

"D'you think anyone's here?" she asked her counsel, half-thrilled, half-terrified.

Paine's head turned swiftly. "No, but...I'm not sure."

They passed the airport and saw two sizable ponds on either side of the road. Paine thought that maybe somehow these reservoirs were the cause of the area's lushness, for he was reluctant to consider Faith's suggestion that a person resided here. That notion frightened him, and his mindset shifted from that moment on.

Past the ponds and on the right appeared the first building. It was a dull orange ranch-style schoolhouse linked to a chapel, covered with blue roofing, and curved around an empty lot. High on the outermost extension of the edifice, in faded white letters, read "Aquinas." Faith saw this and smiled. Now *that's* more like it, she thought. It reminded her of Boston.

Playing fields came after the school and the road curved slightly left before entering the core of the town. They drove past residences with overgrown lawns and toys and balls strewn about. Besides the neglect and rust, the community looked much as it did when its inhabitants were alive: orderly and safe.

The town was sizable, and every inch an oasis. Its

location was even more remote than that of C—, more alone and in need of fending for itself, and as such its ambitions had been commanded forth without sympathy in a way that C—'s never were. C— was a moon, but this town was its own planet.

To Faith, the town was welcoming, and she hoped Paine felt this, too; it was handsome and pleasant but clearly the product of an uncompromising, potent initiative. The aura of its surface exuded a happy discontent. Throughout its history, the more the town achieved in rectifying itself, the more sense the possibilities provided the community.

Faith stopped the vehicle at the intersection of D Street. A quick glance was all she needed for an accurate, intuitive assessment that this was formerly the center of the community, both culturally and economically. She put the car in park, turned off the engine, and exited frenetically. Paine moved much slower, reaching into the back seat before opening his door.

"*Hello!*" she shouted into the air. A bird flew overhead and behind a square building. Nothing else moved. "*HELL-OOOO!*" she screamed again, a shrill flooding through the town in every direction, reverberating in every arcade without echo. Paine stood shielded by his open door. He gripped the stock, slid the pump, took rounds from the glove box, and fingered the magazine tube.

Faith walked away, then turned to Paine. He appeared from behind the vehicle, and the sight of him with the shotgun surprised her. "D'you think somebody's here?"

"I still don't know," he answered. "Just be cautious."

"I will."

But she did not arm herself. What she imagined was a survivor, like her, not a lost man, and briefly resented her counsel. She felt safe with Paine and thought he should feel safe, too, and did not want to believe that the town harbored a murderer. The town was too endearing, almost beckoning to make her acquaintance—she refused to ruin the feeling she had with thoughts of a potential underside. This she was happy to delegate to Paine, and thought maybe he deserved it.

She would wait to explore; for now she would extract fuel from the well at the gas station. At the back of the trailer she opened the latched door. To the left were a dozen Jerry cans, half of which were empty. She bowed her head under the strap of a duffel bag.

Paine stalked the street, more confused than he had felt in a long time. Unlike his ward, he sensed something was amiss in the town. On outward appearance, the town was certainly welcoming, even charming, but he could not ignore the intense sensation of eidetic messages he felt it was struggling to convey. Whether or not someone was here, he did not know, but he knew death intimately. The aura of charisma was logically unexplainable. To Paine it felt baggy, like sheep's clothing.

Faith began the process. Working a crowbar with two hands and one foot, she popped open the heavy, rusted cap and flipped it over onto the concrete. She unraveled a braid of yarn tied at one end to a dumbbell. She lowered the weight inch by inch down the well until it went slack, then retrieved it hand over fist. She pinched her thumb on the dip mark and held the slimy weight in front of her like the head of Medusa. It swayed as she lowered it to the ground. She picked up a bottle by the handle, spun its cap, and processed some loose math. She remembered her father teaching her how to restore fuel, memories that morphed into thoughts of the one. *Two more days*, she said to herself.

Paine stopped before a tattered awning that read *Thorpe Opera House*. He shuddered. He felt something bad was going to happen and was wondering why no visions were presenting themselves. Though sandwiched between two connected buildings, the brick theater seemed lonely and vacuous. Holding the shotgun under his arm and with his finger on the trigger, he reached with his left hand to pull open the door.

He took a careful look inside. The sun lit a triangular patch on the floor. The rest was terminally black. There were no windows; it was a darkness not meant to be shared. The silence inside sounded hollow and angry.

*   *

"That's it for now," she declared when he reappeared, then slammed shut the door of the trailer. "Did you find anything?"

His face looked cold. "No."

"Did you find any*one*?" she asked with a half-hearted smile, as if it were a hackneyed joke.

He shook his head. She did not need to look up to know the answer.

She wiped her hands on her pants. "What was that noise? It sounded like broken glass."

He fidgeted for a more casual way to hold the shotgun. "No...I mean, yes, I...I entered the building on the corner, but the door locked behind me. I had to get out through a window." He gazed back at where he had been.

"Oh." She stretched her arms over her head, then dropped them suddenly. "Is that blood?" She focused intently on one of his hands. "Are you bleeding?"

He looked down at himself. "No, I...yes, you're right. I didn't notice. I must have cut myself on the glass when I climbed out."

"Let me see that. It looks pretty bad." She came closer. "You must've really gashed yourself."

He pulled his hand up his sleeve, a few inches. "It's alright—I see it. It's just a small cut. I'll wrap it up

David A. Colón

myself." He shuffled to the vehicle, his mind blank; she stared down the street, at nothing in particular.

*   *

It took Faith almost an entire day to get over her frustration with Paine. They left the town so abruptly that, per his request, he drove while she ate. He told her he was sure that they were alone but, nonetheless, they did not belong there: through a sense he would not classify as a vision, he realized exploring the town was in a way undermining their greater scheme—to quest for the one. She agreed, even though she thought that somewhere he was lying.

She believed the town had much to offer, but perhaps a fantasy and a longing were good enough. Sometimes a bite is more gratifying than a fill, especially for Paine, who had rubbed off on her over the years.

They found their way back to Interstate 80. The plan was to drive a few hours and set camp, but Paine could not sleep and so he drove until dawn. Faith stayed awake for much of the way, insisting it was not for company but safety in the night. Her mind buzzed with aggressive thoughts repressed by her temporary displeasure for her companion. She reclined her seat and slept peacefully for many hours, during which time Paine stole more than a few admiring glances. She awoke with perfect timing, he thought, for he was gleeful to make amends by welcoming her to Salt Lake City.

Six

At an hour past sunrise, Mann was speeding in a pickup truck on a return trip to the ranch. The list of remaining preparations was short, short enough to keep in his head. La Maison was immaculate, accommodations meticulously prepared, and the kitchen primed for the work of cooking the banquet. Already the weather promised a beautiful day.

His mind spun like a gyroscope, the thoughts never wobbling; every fancy he had had of the one cycled around and around without tiring. Once he had a dream of them both as children, romping in a field of tall grass and ignoring each other the way little boys and girls do when they play sometimes; and the dream ended with her calling his attention to a poppy she picked and offered as a gift. This reverie meshed with more likely visions: braiding her hair as she sat swelled with child, being summoned from the fields to rest and share supper.

Mann had food on the mind, and was delighted to present his affections by the feast. Like multiplication tables, the menu was exactly memorized. Almost everything was stocked in the kitchen and pantry. He needed only a few more things.

The truck pulled up to the sty Mann himself built many years ago. He removed a large bucket with a smaller pail inside and a long twine cord from the bed of the vehicle.

The Lost Men

There was a shoat, a piglet, farrows, sows, and boars, some lying lazily and some standing still. Once he entered the pen he tied the rope into a harness around the shoulders of the smaller of the two big males and pulled him along.

They headed straight for the forest. Mann slapped the animal's portly underside and said, "Come on, Marquis, pick me a winner." All the pigs had names; they were the only animals smart enough to answer to them. The swine walked with his signature gait, all hooves treading in line as if carrying his fat mass on a balance beam.

The sun passed over almost twenty degrees in the sky, but Mann knew beforehand that this would probably take at least an hour. *So long as The Marquis holds up*, it was no matter. *This will definitely be worth it.* Though as time went on, his hopes for each tree grew.

His thoughts had drifted when Marquis made the discovery. Several feet from the base of a sequoia, Marquis began to dig with his snout and front hooves, almost slyly, as if hiding from notice. Mann pulled on the leash and incited a struggle. Marquis snorted with a chirping whistle, shaking with resistance but too tired to win. Mann tied the rope taut around a nearby branch and went to unearth his treasure.

He scraped the ground with his hands, knowing not to use a spade; this could stab the prize and ruin it. "Excellent," he said loudly. "Oh, perfect." He held three lime-sized black truffles, and these were just the top of the nest.

The final count was twenty-six, the largest almost as big as his fist. The good omens were mounting. Marquis was agitated and wanted to eat, so Mann used this to rein him back to the farm. He untied the twine from the branch and trotted away, dropping a couple of the truffles behind as a lure. Marquis followed desperately.

At the clearing was a metal structure about seven feet

tall, with a large pulley at the top and a giant reel down low. Mann stood next to it and tossed more truffles at his feet. "There, get your fill, boy," he said to the pig, who waddled over, weak in the knees, and munched the first.

Giving a little slack, Mann ran the leash over the pulley and looped the end around the lower reel before securing a complicated knot. He grabbed the hand crank and turned it several clicks, then stopped. Marquis was eating the last truffle. "Okay, one more." Mann dropped another bulb under his snout. He chewed it busily and, before swallowing it all, raised his head to see what was going on.

Mann gave his back to the animal and spread his feet in a lunging stance. With both hands he began straining to turn the crank. Suddenly the pig was lifted off its front quarters. It squealed loudly. He turned the crank three more revolutions and then the resistance was much greater. The swine was lifted into the air, the hoarse shouts panicking faster.

Mann turned the wheel until his hands hurt. When he faced the boar it was dangling in the air, the front legs spread apart from the purposeful noose he fashioned at the start. He steadied the pig, then took the pail filled with truffles out of the larger plastic bucket, which he precisely placed beneath the hanging swine. Off the ground he picked up a massive knife, long as a machete and menacingly serrated, walked next to the pig, grabbed its far ear, and sawed its throat open with one powerful tug of the blade.

The yelp could be heard for miles. Aether surged through the animal, spasms rattling the carriage, hips gyrating in the air. He stared at the white plastic as it was splashed with maroon blood. He had two things on his mind: the crisped skin of a roast, and black sausage for breakfast. In time, he returned to La Maison and completed six hours of cooking. To him, there was such a difference between the soul of a man and the life of an animal that he failed to make any connection at all between survival and murder.

*   *

A quick exchange with Joy revealed that the one's arrival was to be expected soon. Before she left the room she hugged him kindly, squeezing his hands with the emotion of a nanny in the service of an absent mother.

He closed the door behind her and stood alone in his bedroom. With nostalgia his eyes ran up and around the spacious chamber. He grasped that nothing will be the same. It was possible, even likely, that this companion would accompany him the rest of his days. Seven years of solitude and eight years of counsel had but two hours to live. There was no fear anymore, just a sober awareness of an era's final gasps. In a sense, as he alone embodied nearly half a percent of the world's survivors, the magnitude of this forthcoming union was on the scale of nations in the age of population.

On his bed laid a suit six generations old. It, a shirt, and tie were carefully bagged in transparent plastic. He slid his hand over his freshly shaven face and approached the long mirror to inspect his complexion. He pulled on the skin of his neck, then removed his bathrobe.

There was nothing to try to do now. His education, his life, the personality that had taken firm shape were there, and he felt nothing but assured. For the first time he reflected on his worth, and realized he felt confident to think that he was a good man. He removed the plastic guards gingerly from the clothes and began to dress himself, putting his arms through the sleeves of the shirt and threading the buttons from the top down.

Struck by a flash of spontaneity, he joyfully submitted.

David A. Colón

The silence was unnecessary. Now was the perfect time to rehearse that most ardent sermon *For Preventing the Children of Poor People in Ireland from being a Burden to their Parents or Country, and For making them Beneficial to the Public.*

Mann reached for his tie and returned to the mirror. He cleared his voice, turned up his collar, and spoke forcefully.

*   *

Half an hour later he fastened the last cufflink, pleased his recitation was flawless. He was certain that no extant text revealed more about the age of population. His complacency doubled. Posing plainly in the mirror, he shot his cuffs, and marveled at how his great-great-great grandfather was exactly the same size as he.

*   *

Joy placed her book down and took a breath. "You look perfectly handsome."

"Do I? Thank you. Although this shirt is terribly itchy."

"You'll sweat and it will feel better." She noticed half his collar was untucked but did not get up to offer to fix it. "I could hear you upstairs. Were you reciting something?"

"*A Modest Proposal.*"

She shrugged and tucked her hands between her thighs. "That text has become quite an intimate friend of yours."

He was too anxious to sit. "And I thank you for introducing me to it."

She closed her eyes. "You remember well. That was many years ago."

He looked at the fireplace. "And it has haunted me ever since."

The Lost Men

"Haunted?"

"Have you forgotten?" he asked. "Have you forgotten what it says?"

She tucked a strand of hair behind her ear. "Some of the details, yes."

He projected his voice. "'A child just dropped from its dam may be supported by her milk for a solar year, with little other nourishment; at most not above the value of two shillings, which the mother may certainly get, or the value in scraps, by her lawful occupation of begging; and it is exactly at one year old that I propose to provide for them in such a manner as instead of being a charge upon their parents or the parish, or wanting food and raiment for the rest of their lives, they shall on the contrary contribute to the feeding, and partly to the clothing, of many thousands.'"

"Mm." Her lips were pursed.

"'I have been assured by a very knowing American of my acquaintance in London, that a young healthy child well nursed is at a year old a most delicious, nourishing, and wholesome food, whether stewed, roasted, baked, or boiled; and I make no doubt that it will equally serve in a fricassee or a ragout.'"

She squirmed. "I have indeed forgotten much."

He gently tugged his sleeves. "'The famous Psalmanazar, a native of the island Formosa, who came from thence to London above twenty years ago, and in conversation told my friend, that in his country when any young person happened to be put to death, the executioner sold the carcass to persons of quality as a prime dainty; and that in his time the body of a plump girl of fifteen, who was crucified for an attempt to poison the emperor, was sold to his imperial majesty's prime minister of state, and other great mandarins of the court, in joints from the gibbet.'"

Her eyes smiled; her lips frowned. "That is brutal."

He fidgeted more with his clothes. "It has a hold on me."

"Are you planning to recite it at the banquet?"

"Yes, I hope to."

Her eyes followed him as he paced. "It might be too morbid."

"But it's a *satire*," he declared, the word punched out in a husky whisper. "People actually *laughed* at it once. That's part of its lesson; that's part of my point."

"I understand, but, still."

"Well, if the one can appreciate intensity, as I assume she can—gathered from what you've told me—then she'll more than stomach it."

"It's gruesome." Her ken was unflappable, as if a dictionary could speak. "And I'm not sure if she shares your appreciation for intensity."

He ambled back from the window. "She, she." He flexed the word, a prosthesis. "If she can't see what's worth knowing about *A Modest Proposal*, well...I couldn't even imagine."

Joy pulled her feet up to the couch, to her side. "Maybe she won't," she reiterated.

"Well then maybe I'll make her," he countered swiftly, more like a child than a chauvinist.

"I wonder if you should herald such depraved images."

"Why not? My reason is not vulgar entertainment; I hope to cast light on the important beliefs we must uphold."

"And the practice of murder you think is obsolete? Lest you forget the lost men."

Mann froze. "But that's different. You're getting beside the point."

"I disagree." She crossed her arms. "There are those in this world who still do kill. And if it is fate to confront them, in any circumstance we could foresee, how should they be met? With kindness? With tolerance?"

He sighed. "You pose an exercise in the abstract. The one is concrete; our union is concrete."

"That is my point," she interrupted. "The fact of murder is not something to share without provocation. There is no place for killing, or killers, in our existence, the life and duty of survival. The seed of evil is planted at birth and manifest in actions. Lost men kill because it is their fate, not ours. But, unless..."

"What?"

She lifted her posture. "If faced with the threat of our own murder, how should we react?"

"What do you mean?"

"Would we be justified in killing another if we knew his intention was to kill us?"

He resumed pacing. "That I don't know."

"Of course we would," she said, and leaned forward. "Lost men are not persuaded; they are of death's essence, the damned; they are born to be who they are; they do not reason their way to a decision to kill—it is their impulse, it is, for them, a version of what for us is survival."

"So you say that a killer should be put to death by our own hand? You puzzle me. Wouldn't that then make *us* lost men? Would that not bring into question our own fates?"

"No. Our charge is to survive. Taking the life of a lost man in order to preserve mankind is an unfortunate circumstance, perhaps a moral dilemma, but not a definitive trait. There is a vast difference—the vastest difference—between a violent act of survival and a random, senseless murder. It is a question of motive. Motive is what defines humanity."

He looked up to the ceiling. "How can anyone know? Who really knows the mind of a lost man? Who knows the limit, the fine line, the border between hope and the void?"

"There is no mind to explore; the lost man has no conscience. A lost man is lost from the start. Why, I do not know. But history has proven this true. And perhaps the saddest truth is that more will come; more will be born. It is our penance, the paradox of our existence—that we will birth ones destined to take life."

"As has always been."

"As has always been."

He finally sat. "What will become of us?"

She shook her head. "I will know in time."

"Will we succeed? Will we make a better life? Am I grounded, am I founded, to believe in what I think and know is right?"

She spoke softly. "There is no evil in you. Or...rather..." She blinked. "There is no more evil in you than is in any natural man."

He stared at her. "There is evil in all of us, is there not?"

She smiled sadly. "Hence our condition."

He stood again. "I've always known this. Perhaps this is why *A Modest Proposal* appeals to me so."

"No," she objected, "it is not for evil; its appeal is to your sense of ethics."

He scratched his ear. "Well, I'll reconsider my recitation. Certain dark matters, I agree, need not be explored."

She touched her neck. "Not without due cause."

"And the determined lives of the unborn, I agree, will test the bounds of our ethics."

"It is a constant of life."

He stood perfectly still. "There is no reason in the mystery. Good will breed evil; the precious, cheapened; and hopelessness will turn to praise; and the unspoken will someday be law."

The Lost Men

She gazed at him with pride.

He turned his back to the light. "It's getting late; she must be here soon, no?"

Joy closed her eyes. "Yes, she will."

"Are you ready?" he asked.

"Of course."

He glanced out the doorway. "I can feel her." He took a few steps before laying eyes on the tome beside his counsel.

"And what were *you* reading?" he asked.

She placed her hand on the book without looking. "Revelation."

*   *

Paine and Faith slept late. The uncommon tranquility of their surroundings cleared their minds and kept them at rest until mid-morning. They had set camp on the center lawn of an ornately decorated Buddhist compound, and Faith's giddiness, feeding exchanges filled with laughter about the Bodhisattva and the Happy Buddha, had kept the two awake until the late hours. A rare occurrence, in the morning she arose before her counsel and had to wake him with some effort.

In the brook behind the temple, Faith bathed more intensely than she was aware of. With the aid of sunlight, she was able to search the compound's rooms for help in her presentation—and was wildly successful. She found a jade hair clip in the gift shop and pinned her silken locks in a bun with a sprig of sweet-smelling lavender. When she emerged from the monastery she was dressed in a pink sleeveless shirt of a golden eye design, a burgundy meditation skirt tied in the front, and hemp sandals.

"You look beautiful!" Paine exclaimed.

"So will *you*," she said, extending a hanger draped with

David A. Colón

another outfit of clothes. He let out an embarrassed laugh, embarrassed a bit for both of them, for neither had had any idea this would be the first foot they would put forward when meeting the one.

*   *

Paine drove them through the lushness of California, winding along mountainsides with breathtaking views. Faith sat in silence, knowing her counsel was continuously guided by flitting visions that required attention. For hours they rode without saying a word. She struggled to suppress memories of Salt Lake City—the life she had lived, defined by reflecting on experiences to mine them for wisdom, was compromising her budding efforts to welcome the future.

Spineless cacti spotted the terrain. The vehicle felt much lighter without the trailer. They left almost everything they had beside the Buddhist compound, knowing their destination wanted for nothing.

The closer they got, the less the world mattered. The Pacific Ocean, the San Francisco Bay: nothing was said. On either side of the highway were countless buildings and signs, all unique in style to the area, but still they remained quiet. Faith rubbed the sweat of her palms on her skirt. Paine exited the freeway without announcement.

"This is it," he said calmly. "Welcome to..." he began, then paused. He wanted to say *The House of Being* but that could not be right. "...your new home."

They made two turns into a residential area before entering a hidden driveway. The vehicle slowly ascended the brick road to an iron gate. It stood open and hinged on two stone columns topped with urn finials nearly twenty feet high. The sense of awe was imposing. It took another minute before they passed the carport on the right and pulled to a stop in front of La Maison. But so long a wait was to end far more suddenly.

Mann and Faith opened their doors at the same time. She exited the vehicle; he stood in the threshold.

Their eyes met.

They felt the same. Just to see another person was surreal enough: but to know what this meant was too enormous for any mind. He studied her movements and form, and no comparisons came. He could not believe it and yet everything was true. She was there. She was *here*. And she was his.

Faith strode up the stone stairs, her dam of composure breached by waves of tears. Mann stepped forward and their bodies collided. She cried into his shoulder as if she held in her arms the ghost of her father. His eyes were firmly shut and he squeezed her body with violent tenderness. This was infinitely better than the self-possessed introduction he had envisioned and rehearsed, and he fell madly in love before even knowing her name.

Seven

Introducing the counsels was an exercise in overstimulation. The euphoria of meeting the one consumed every feeling, thought, and word, yet there were more people to account for: encounters that alone would have been almost as portentous. But the responsibilities of the future were not delegated equally among the four, so the counsels shadowed the event, relegated as strikingly prominent afterthoughts.

Faith stopped crying though her eyes continued to glisten, as did his. Mann adopted the awkward mannerism of touching his hand to her shoulder at each exchanged pleasantry. He felt genuine affection but was stiff and apprehensive, the pairing of a life of loneliness with a desire to make her feel welcome calculating the movements.

"Please come in and sit down," he said, placing his palm high on her back.

The four entered the salon. "Your home is beautiful," she said, her eyes ranging about.

"Thank you," he responded. "But it's *our* home now."

Paine smiled and Joy nodded. In secret she was seeing into the future.

Mann crossed his legs. "I don't know where to begin. There's so much to say and so much to learn about each other."

The Lost Men

"I know," she replied, her tone friendly. "But there's so much time, isn't there?"

"Of course. I feel like my life has just begun."

She loved his voice.

They spoke a short while. He asked about her arduous travels, and she responded stoically. He was eager to hear details though he knew the stories would be better told in intimate company. Some experiences were elaborated and practical matters addressed.

"You reconstitute gasoline to power vehicles?" he asked.

"Yes, with a simple stabilizer."

"That's so interesting. I rely almost exclusively on solar power, although I do have some vehicles that require fuel, but they're all diesel engines converted to use vegetable oil."

"*Really?*"

"Sure. With the right equipment it's a fairly simple mechanical conversion, and unopened vegetable oil, if kept in airtight plastic bottles, the kind you'd find in warehouses and grocery stores, still works perfectly."

It was clear to both that there was much to learn.

Mann interrupted himself. "What am I saying?" he blurted. "You must be famished." He looked at Paine and pointed his hand towards the kitchen. "Why don't we sit in the dining room and start dinner?"

They all agreed.

*   *

"My grandfather was a vintner," Mann said, standing by the head of the table, which was covered in white and set with fine china and silverware. "He lived not far from here, maybe a hundred miles south. He taught the craft to my father. I don't suppose you've ever had wine before, have you?"

David A. Colón

"No," Faith responded, "though my father used to ferment apple cider. And he, my mother, and I drank a bit too much of it the night before they left me." The counsels chuckled forgivingly, and she glanced about and smiled.

"Oh, and did he teach you?"

"Yes he did. It's been a while, but I remember how," she promised.

Mann presented a dark green magnum. "Well this was made by my grandfather over forty years ago. I keep many of these in my cellar." He fitted a corkscrew into the top, opened it, and poured everyone a glass.

"A toast: to life, and what's yet to come," he said staring into Faith's eyes.

"In wine there is truth," Joy added.

"And in time there is youth," Paine retorted.

There was a confused pause before Paine shrugged, sparking boisterous laughter from them all. They drank, and Mann was thrilled at the quality.

He excused himself and entered the kitchen. The counsels spoke to each other. Faith looked up at the electric lights. They hum-buzzed in a way that almost made her feel like she was on another planet.

He returned with a serving cart topped with steaming bowls. "Soup," he declared. He served his guests first, himself last. Under turbid broth, cheek filet on softened shallots, topped with a charcoal fan of sliced truffle.

"Gorgeous," Faith said. It was the word she felt the most.

Mann sat and placed a napkin on his lap. "So, Faith, may I ask if you have a favorite book?"

The unusual flavors of the soup were distracting, but she responded. "Well, that's a difficult question. I don't think I've ever read a book that I didn't find noteworthy."

"I know what you mean."

"But some do stand out from the rest. Many epics, and

of course religious scriptures, but the moral romance for me is the happiest compromise of the two, so if I had to find a book that contained within it all the pleasure I get from reading it would probably be a moral romance."

Mann wiped his mouth. "Have you read *Rasselas*?"

Faith looked astonished. "*Yes*," she said, and stiffened her back. "That is precisely the book I had in mind."

He gave a magisterial nod. "I've just been rereading it this week, in fact."

"It offers *so much*," she said with zeal.

The counsels made eye contact.

He took a gulp of wine. "'Knowledge will always predominate over ignorance, as man governs the other animals.'"

"True," she said. "And 'there is little to be feared from the malevolence of men, and yet less to be hoped from their affection or esteem.'"

"*Ha!*" he barked. "I take issue with the latter, and I bet you do, too. At least I *hope* you do!" he said spiritedly, and she agreed with a gentle expression.

"That's what I call the Tao of Dr. Johnson," she joked.

"Ha, that's good," he muttered as he returned to folding his soup. "Well, in the spirit of our acquaintance, remember that 'Marriage is evidently the dictate of nature; men and women are made to be companions of each other; and therefore I cannot be persuaded but that marriage is one of the means of happiness.'"

She swallowed a bite. "Not terribly subtle: 'Man cannot so far know the connection of causes and events as that he may venture to do wrong in order to do right.'"

Mann squinted, pursed his lips, and looked at her. "That's very, very true." After a moment's reflection he resumed eating.

Joy, delighted at the jocular banter, was impressed with the girl. They ate more. "How is your soup?" she asked politely.

Faith sighed. "It's delicious. I've never eaten meat I could cut with my spoon. I've never tasted anything like it."

"Good," Mann said and looked to Paine, who adamantly concurred, though he had no idea.

*   *

The next course was salad, a small pile of spinach, carrot, almonds, plum, and endive. Mann explained it was inspired by the Chinese five-color style.

"It looks like a little tropical island," Faith remarked, feeling almost guilty to destroy it with her fork.

"Thank you," he said coyly. "Enjoy."

Paine found restraint difficult. He struggled to eat at the same slow pace as the others.

"You know," Mann began, "what you said before about causes and events when we were discussing *Rasselas* really has me thinking." He paused in contemplation. "Considering the events of the world, in other words our history, of all of them what do you think was most important?"

"What do you mean?" Faith asked. "Do you *really* mean of all the world's events, which do I think was most important?"

"I know it's...well, in a word, yes."

She sniffed. "The hardest questions are always the easiest to ask."

"Well I ask because I'm certain it's open for debate. Though I do have my opinions."

This captivated her. "You do?"

"I do."

"Then let's have them," she suggested gleefully. By this point everything was relaxed and cordial.

Mann chewed his salad and swallowed. "I'd have to say it was the economic collapse."

Faith almost choked. "Are you *serious?*"

"Absolutely."

Faith was stunned with disbelief. She glanced at Joy, then turned to Mann. "Why would you say that?"

Mann wiped his mouth with the napkin. "For many reasons. You must know how deeply dependent the world was on money."

"Certainly. I don't think that's open for debate."

"Of course; it was undoubtedly the Age of Money. And from what was documented in newspapers of the economic collapse we can see how soon after it the world entered its demise. After the collapse it was but a month before the urban purges, and then printing presses ceased publication, government agencies shut down, industry ceased, universities closed, soldiers deserted—it's like civilization just vanished."

Faith sipped more wine, which grew on her with every taste. "I read the periodicals, too, and those events are undeniable, but you accept the premise that the collapse was a beginning. Pardon my frankness, but it smacks of post-hoc fallacy."

Mann was not offended. "I respect your objection." He, too, drank. "But I'm afraid I won't be able to defend my position on the centrality of money in the age of population without invoking a tiresome litany of citations."

"That won't be necessary," she said forgivingly. "I already said I agree on that point."

He paused.

"Could you imagine living in a world with money?"

She returned his look and shook her head.

He held her gaze. "Money's greatest accomplishment was rendering all people unequal."

Faith finished her salad and leaned back in her chair.

David A. Colón

"Mann, I think in the events of the final decades of population there were so many phenomena, so many manifestations of civilization's decay—the collapse was certainly dramatic, but whether it was a cause or a result is so uncertain to me. Before the collapse there were so many indications of demise: terrorism and *its* dramatic effects, the wars between the East and the West, the impunity of actions by corrupt politicians, the intolerance of religious differences, the proliferation of technologies that dispensed with entire labor forces, exhausting the planet of its natural resources...I feel I could go on and on, and they're all of the same character as the economic collapse, all circumstances of administration and confusion. I think that no aspect of the demise of population can be classified as the world's most important event, for it really was, simply, inexplicable."

Mann propped his head with his fist. "And why would you say that?"

"Well, for one, none of them explain the patent psychic transformation that humankind underwent. I mean," she said, pointing her hands, palms up, at the two counsels, "how would you explain *them?*"

Mann responded, "Clairvoyance is well documented throughout history and literature: the Oracle of Delphi, the witches of *Macbeth*, Nostradamus, Rasputin..." He also remembered Latimer from *The Lifted Veil*.

"And since at least the Age of Reason they had commonly been regarded as kooks," she retorted. "But do *you* believe they're kooks?"

He shook his head. "Not in the least. We could not survive without them."

"So you'd say that that segment of society that regarded them as false was misguided or naïve?"

"Perhaps I would."

"Okay," she said. "So psychics have always existed.

And their existence today is less an emergence than a liberation." Joy grinned graciously; Paine realized he ate his salad with the wrong fork. "But how then do you explain their inordinate number relative to our surviving population? And how do you explain the personal transformations they experience in their own lifetimes? I assume Joy's personal history resembles Paine's—having loved and lost, having exchanged one of the five senses for the sixth?"

Joy closed her eyes and nodded behind her folded hands.

Faith resumed. "Both of my parents had counsels. Each of my grandparents had a counsel. Paine had a counsel. He tells me each of *his* relations had a counsel. What earthly event could explain this pervasive turn to the supersensory?"

"I couldn't feign a response."

"Neither could I," Faith added. "And yet, in the context of our discussion, if we can agree that life has gone on and that we are still within the continuum of humanity in spite of a lack of historical record, our survival's dependence on these individuals dignifies another candidate for the world's most important event: the emergence of counsels." She paused and looked down. "In fact, that reveals my inclination towards the subject. I'm inclined to consider, in answering your question, those events that do not try to explain the demise of population but rather promise hope; that insinuate a future of optimism, for they not only reconcile the past with the present but also provide a motivation for us in preparing for what may be yet to come."

Mann was fascinated, quite comfortable in defeat. This was what he had lacked in his life. "So do you believe it was the emergence of counsels?" His tone had noticeably changed.

"No," she answered. "The first idea I had after you

asked the question is still the one I believe. I would say it was the Crucifixion."

"Perfectly acceptable. But why?"

"I risk being obvious."

"Hardly."

She touched her fingers to the tablecloth, endeavored to be brief. "For the model of supreme human conduct Christ embodied, whose conviction was immortalized through the trials of the Crucifixion; for the doctrine it spawned through the New Testament, which transformed the identity of Judaism forever and provided the rudiments of Islam..."

He kept watching, so she kept on.

"...for its formation of ideologies, both virtuous and tyrannical, that proliferated throughout the world as religion and empire; for this legacy's role as a motivation for achievement and the glory of humankind; and, perhaps more than anything, for the promise of redemption of our race through the Resurrection and Revelation, when the messiah will return and order all living beings according to their moral worth." She had much more to say but decided that Mann would question points of his choosing.

"And are you a believer? I mean, do you have faith in the messiah?"

"No," she responded. "The story of redemption I appreciate for its allegory."

"It's hard to believe blindly in any story from the past, is it not?"

She nodded with a sympathetic smile. "That's true. I feel the final lesson of Christianity is that, if ethically grounded, we have every reason to view the future with hope."

Everyone's plates were empty. "So if I'm right, you read religious scripture for its moral lessons and its regard for the future as essentially hopeful and just?"

"That's right."

"And you disregard religious rites and ceremonies of worship?"

"Precisely."

"You see," he began, "I, too, have studied scripture and found the lessons of moral instruction valuable, but I never believed that redemption was reserved for the ethically minded. Correct me if I'm wrong, but isn't redemption promised to the believers?"

"Without question," she admitted.

"Without question," he parroted. He was troubled for many reasons, at least a few regarding how she mirrored his own solipsism when interpreting old ideas to suit his inclinations. "If the believers are those to be saved, then even us well-intentioned moralists are condemned."

There was a heavy silence.

"Which would make perfect sense, wouldn't it?" he asked them all. "And yet who could bear living under such unforgiving auspices?" He pinched the bridge of his nose. "I think we all can agree that the circumstances of our existence have obviated the need for worship."

"I agree," she added. "The shepherd needs a flock, no?"

"All of it, all of it," he replied, exasperated, waving his hand, tired of the topic. There were too many churches once, too many doctrines once, too many lines of inference pretending to trace recourse to the single truth of existence. "But the Crucifixion's a good choice. There's no doubting its impact on civilization, and I see how the allegory extends to the present." He stood to punctuate the end of the conversation, and humbly cleared the plates.

*   *

"What is this?" Faith asked.

Mann served the others. "Tartare. I've taken the liberty

of dressing it with olives, leeks, and fennel—I hope you don't mind."

She was still puzzled. Joy noticed. "It's uncooked beef with egg yolk."

"It's raw?"

"Yes."

"Oh," Faith said. "We used to have this all the time. But instead of tartare I called it *wet wood*," she kidded.

Mann smiled; the others giggled. He earned trust with a brief history of tartare's Mongolian roots, and the one watched him mix the dish before doing the same to hers. Once Joy was eating, Paine looked about skittishly before scooping half the portion into his straining mouth.

"Tonight, if you're not too tired, I'll show you around La Maison, but I'll save a proper tour of the grounds for tomorrow."

"That would be perfect," Faith agreed. She paid compliments to Mann's estate and they began to discuss the workings of his everyday life. Wine was poured again and again, the conversation shifted from agriculture to art collecting, and courses were served with increasing celebration: a sauté of cactus, pork belly, and mushrooms; bay mussels in butter wine; lamb stewed in eggplant. Little was made of their vicarious globetrotting as they sopped the juices of every corner of the world. The company and pageantry of the feast were successful, draping their solitude with a veneer of tasteful sophistication. But still the scene was oddly misplaced, like Englishmen dressed for tea in the bush.

"You live the life of a governor," Faith chimed.

Mann put down his glass. "Well, I don't know about *that*, but...the responsibilities *are* persistent."

Everything was tinged with humor.

"You're being modest," she said, weakly gathering her composure. "I think you rule 'La Maison' with..." Her voice broke into laughter, and she covered her mouth with her napkin.

"With *what?*" he chuckled, as did the others.

"With an iron soup ladle," Paine deadpanned. The room boomed with laughter, even from Joy. Mann raised his glass in a mocking toast, and the happy group gradually quieted.

"There's really not much to it," he resumed. "I merely meet the demands of life as I see fit."

Faith asked, "So you think this life is natural?"

"Well, not totally, but in a way it *is* perfectly natural."

"*What* is?"

"Everything about my life here."

She looked at him with honesty; the wine had taken effect. "The ordering of the grounds, your ranches, your garden, your art collection...?"

"It's natural for human life," he replied. "For a life lived in our condition."

"But I mean *besides* this condition," she retorted. A thought entered her mind. "Do you think we, as people, must live in an ordered state?"

Mann paused. "What sort of 'state' do you mean—a government or an environment?"

"Well, what difference does that make?" she countered. "When it comes to ordering people, those are the same, no?"

"With the world as it is, I think that order is achieved by means of, as I said, the demands of survival. But I don't think that's what you mean. Do you mean if the world was populated once again?"

"Yes."

Mann looked to his lap. "I think that depends on numbers. Do you mean thousands or millions or billions?"

"Millions," she replied. "Billions."

He rubbed his face and sighed. "I think the organization

of government would have to emerge organically, based on social mores, et cetera, in order to function harmoniously."

"You mean the masses would have to *believe* in the system of government, or more than that: that they would actually need to devise it themselves via consensus?"

"Well, in a sense...I mean more that the formation of government would have to happen incrementally, and really without a firm imposition of envisioning the whole of a state all at once."

"Unlike, say, the founding of the United States?"

"Yes."

Paine burped silently.

"Then you envision an evolution of, say, treaties that would eventually develop into a body of government?"

He nodded, and spoke a little louder than before. "Perhaps something like that, in a particular scenario. But I don't think that 'treaties' is the right word. It would be more like *agreements*, not legislation per se for that would necessitate a legislative body, but something more towards an amalgam of agreed-upon actions that would offer a shared code of conduct."

"That sounds very democratic," she noted.

"In a way. But democracy implies bureaucracy, and that's not what I suggest. I think the ideal political situation would be one in which laws were conceived in the broadest terms and administered by regarding the core spirit, if you will, of the purpose and common good of the laws, and only with time would they be narrowed and focused if circumstances dictated it."

"So really you envision a moral form of government?"

"Yes, I think that's the closest thing to it. It would have to be moral because I *do* think that there's no place for a penal system in society. So long as there's no system of money, and ethics are featured prominently to ensure humane treatment of all people, then social agreements on the standards of good behavior could conceivably function successfully to order society without penal threat."

"But how would these agreements be reached? Democratically?"

"Again, I wouldn't use the term 'democratically' because of democracy's history. Democracy, like communism, was a myth. I think the kinds of agreements that I envision would be reached not democratically but *organically*; given shared circumstances, even when the interests of opposed parties would be in disagreement, the compromises that most benefit all parties involved would be achieved, for without a legislative body and without a penal system, arbitration would de facto be achieved through dialogue—through agreement."

"So your form of ideal government would be minimal and uninstitutionalized?"

"Yes."

"A form of anarchy?"

Mann balked, then conceded the point. "I think that's right: a form of anarchy. You see, I used to think that *totalitarianism* was in fact the ideal form of government—one individual, ethically grounded and edified, could compose the right rules of conduct for the people to adopt, but I realized that this would unavoidably breed a species of religious worship, the worship of the totalitarian, and religion in all its incarnations of worship would be a destructive force against the growth of fair government."

"So the organic emergence of social controls, born from an anarchic state, is what you deem the most ideal system of government?"

"If you could call it 'government.' I think of it more as the *replacement* of government: moral, as you mentioned. I mean, consider this: without a system of money to generate social inequity, without a penal system to threaten the lives of citizens, and without the doctrines of religion to breed factions, then what is there for people to live for?"

Faith replied, "Rectification of the self for the common good."

"*Exactly*." He stood complacently, a feeling of harmony she shared. But in truth, what seemed to them a confident resolution was in fact dangerous. As forebears of the hopes for humanity, the two were better suited to disagree on such abstract matters. Every opinion they shared expensed contrary propositions, thus pruning the topics of debate for their progeny.

He cleared the plates again and entered the kitchen. Faith smiled at the counsels. He returned with the serving cart covered with melon, figs, and two large roasts. "It's time to stop being so dainty," he quipped.

Faith looked to Paine, who passed her a knowing glance. They both remembered what he had predicted about the one's ability to disarm any person with an unpretentious saying.

Eight

They moved to the salon, and lounged like a pride of lions. Throughout the post-dinner conversation Paine wondered whether Mann was going to play music or not. He thought he would but was wrong.

"Perhaps now is a good time to show you around the house," Mann said. "Joy: when he's ready, will you show Paine to his quarters?"

Both counsels nodded, though they would continue to talk until dawn.

"Shall we?" he asked, offering his hand to Faith. She took it, stood and left with her companion.

He led her through a doorway at the far side of the salon. It opened to a room, dark even after lit. The forest-green walls framed maps of the colonial world, each depicting, in unique ways, borderless frontiers. The two spoke lightly, asking each other small questions. Her wide eyes renewed everything for him. "Joy is quite fond of this room," he commented.

At the end of the room was a threshold leading to another room, and from their vantage they could see the next room led to another, and that room led to another, and another: a portico of five identically sized rooms which looking at felt like gazing into a pair of facing mirrors. From the green den they entered a small art studio, white, with painted canvases leaning in a stack against the wall.

"Are these your paintings?" she asked excitedly.

"Some of them," he replied.

She leafed through the wooden frames. The first was simply a painted spectrum, the colors blended seamlessly together. The next was an ornate design of patterns swirling in baroque billows—the lines yellow, the shading various tints of purple.

"These are beautiful," she said admiringly. "They really are."

He thanked her shyly.

She turned to the next canvas, a mauve still-life of two blue herons drawn to anatomical perfection, though the positioning of their bodies was wholly unnatural.

"Why haven't you framed these and hung them up?"

He shrugged. Painting was the most private thing he ever did, and he was at a loss to express how this publicity made him feel.

"If I may be so bold," she said, "I would like to see these all the time."

He dropped his head and smiled.

They ambled through the arcade—one room featured a billiards table, she thought another's sofas looked very comfortable. Mann led them out a side door to the main corridor.

"This suite will be Paine's quarters." He pushed open the double doors and strode into the apartment. The vaulted ceiling enlarged the living room, kitchen, bedroom, den, and water closet, and in the twilight Faith could see through the window into a wild garden crowned with a trellis.

"This is magnificent," she said. Mann nodded at her approval, and at that moment she knew she would always love him. For all his sophistication, dignity, and talent, he was also considerate and attentive. The efforts he took in preparing for her arrival—from his suit to the feast to the lilac in the vase—were too extensive to ignore, too deep to read without hope. She thought his measures were more than compulsory, for they exceeded her expectations tenfold.

But she was still uncertain as to which of her chief emotional demands Mann would fulfill: to be needed or to be desired. On this matter her intuition and wishes were one and the same. As commanding as he clearly was over his existence, it could only mean that he desired her. And to her that meant the most.

He continued the tour through the kitchen, pantry, and butchery and down a small staircase to the cellar where he lectured on the winemaking process. Faith listened with barely an ear, for her mind lilted to a melody unconcerned with possessions. She wanted to discuss the future with him, but only in her imagination; she would not have changed the subject even if he had offered to. She predicted he would make a good father, and loved him for what she hoped him to be.

* *

Faith had never ridden an elevator before, and as she exited she laughed, "*What an odd sensation!*"

"It goes up to the roof," he said cheerfully, "to the greenhouse. But it's empty. This way."

The two walked down the hallway. He opened doors to the parlor, music room, and guest bathroom, chambers long ago lived in, in turns, by five families.

"And this is the study," he announced.

When they walked in, she gasped. "Is that a *Picasso?*"

"Yes it is," he replied. "And so is that." He pointed.

She glanced about and absorbed the rarity of the room's treasures, recognizing the styles of Klee and Miró, but the first painting reached out to her senses with an irresistible grasp.

"You like this one?"

She walked up to it slowly. The frame was as tall as she, the painting a black and white portrait of a man in fetal position. The cubist style evoked dementia.

"This is brilliant," she whispered.

He was piqued by her preference. He thought the Chagall or Miró would appeal to her more, at least for their color.

This is as close as we can get to people. She stepped closer to the painting and raised her hand. With all five fingers she stroked the glistening surface, deciphering the invisible dimples of brushstrokes as if reading Braille.

Mann winced. Her caress of the canvas was like a brand seared into his face. When he showed his own forgettable experiments, she praised them. When he showed the masterpieces he safeguarded, she groped them. He was frustrated because he had not yet accepted that he was no longer alone.

"May I ask you a question?" he asked.

"Of course."

"What do you know about your ancestors?"

She turned from the painting, looked at him, then glanced at the floor. "Unfortunately I know very little. I only know of my mother's lineage. Her great-great-great grandfather was an Air Force pilot, and *his* mother was a famous actress."

"Really? Such unusual professions."

"*I* think so. How about you?"

"I'm afraid I know as little as you. Let's see: my mother's great-great-great grandfather bought and sold land and buildings, and my father's great-great-great-great-great-great-great"—he counted on his fingers to her amusement—"grandfather was a bootlegger in Chicago in the 1920s."

David A. Colón

She laughed. "*Really?* That history has survived?"

"Yes it has...apparently everyone in my father's family was fond of his legacy."

"*A criminal*," she stated with ersatz gravity.

"Indeed he was."

They looked around the room in different directions, and his emotions sank in the pause. None of the professions mentioned were of any use anymore, and realizing this spoiled what was meant to be fruitful conversation.

They talked about the study's paintings and books for a while, which Mann used as a segue to the library. He opened its doors proudly, expecting her to erupt with enthusiasm, but he did not know that she had once held the last Gutenberg Bible.

"Oh, this is spectacular," she said. "What a collection. How many books do you have here?"

"I think around 80,000. And I spend most of my evenings reading up in that loft." He gestured and her eyes followed.

They looked at each other. She sidestepped the moment. "Mann," she said kindly, all tension in her shoulders released, "what you've done here at La Maison is so honorable. I really mean that."

"Thanks."

For a few seconds he felt like a brother.

"Well," he began, "would you like to peruse, perhaps for some bedroom reading?"

She was a little confused. "Um...that sounds great."

He walked. "The bottom shelves house mostly technical books: carpentry, engineering, chemistry, applied physics. As the shelves ascend: economics, politics, history, art, drama, letters, essays, fiction, poetry, theology, scripture."

She looked to the very top.

He smiled. "Help yourself."

Unsure of what this meant for the rest of the evening,

she complied and strolled ahead, commanding a growing space as she paced the shelves. Mann drifted like a chaperone, paying attention to the silence of her thought processes. After two minutes she went for the ladder and slid it half the length of the room.

Four of Shakespeare's plays and a volume of Dutch impressionist painting. Mann nodded with a happy look. "Great," he said plainly. "I'll show you to your quarters."

He strode a few paces ahead. They went back down the hallway to the end. She observed the way he filled out his suit: hard where it fit, gone where it draped. His decorum returned to formality as he announced before the doors that this was to be hers.

They entered the threshold into a vast living room. The quarters he rationed were a house unto itself. A staircase led down to a lower level and hallways branched into a dozen rooms. They briefly toured the space, down and up, and ended in her bedroom.

"Well, that's it," he said. "You know where everything is."

"Yes."

"Tomorrow I'll be up at dawn. But I hope you'll be sure to rest. After your journey, you must be weakened."

She was at a loss for words.

"Goodnight."

The entry was empty. She listened to his footsteps fade down the hall until the front doors shut, rattling, then silent. On her bed lay the stack of books slid into collapse. She wondered if this was what it would mean to love a man: to know when to trust him and to know when to leave him alone.

*   *

The hours turned into days. On the first he worked

precisely as he had before—interspersed with mealtime conversations, however, which he equally looked forward to and dreaded. The counsels disappeared into the wilderness and there was no telling when they would return. It appeared Joy, too, had coaxed her charge into a new way of doing things.

They slept apart. On the second day Faith arose at dawn and expressed a desire to work. He politely refused by noting again the need for her to rest. But he was lying. In truth, he was protecting his habits from demise, habits which he had not yet realized were as critical to his sanity as to his survival. Disappointed, but with little objection, she graciously acquiesced, spent the afternoon in the bath, and by night had finished both *Hamlet* and *King Lear*.

The following morning they arose in tandem; she offered her services; again he declined. Few words were exchanged over it, and in no time at all she was alone again.

Her mind was a playground, questions swinging to and fro. *Why is he doing this? Does he not want my company? Is he impatient? Scared? Unhappy?* Infested with doubt, she realized this could only mean one thing: he did not trust her. He neither delegated tasks nor welcomed her help, and, in the new circumstance, the isolation was belittling.

She wondered how deep ran his penchant for solitude, for the more they were together the more he exposed how native it was to him. All his gestures of kindness prized individuality: offers of books, sleeping apart, granting time and space for repose.

When she thought about love, she asked: *Does one love another for what one sees of oneself in the other?* If this were true, then maybe his distancing was actually a mode of endearment. Perhaps detachment soothed his emotions, and he assumed it did for her, too. But the truth was inside her feelings, and she could not ignore that, although guarded, she felt unloved.

She decided to do something. She kicked off the slippers Mann gave her, laced her boots, took a compass, and loaded her .44 Carbine. There was no way she would play the house pet. Her habits made demands as well.

A few hours later Mann returned for lunch and was dismayed to find her gone. Cutting corn and cleaning troughs all morning, he thought about countless topics for conversation, mindful of her interests and intending to resuscitate points made over the prior night's dinner. The weight of her company was lightening with every meal, and for the first time he was disappointed to be alone.

Deep in the woods she crouched next to the stump of a fallen tree, a natural cover twenty yards from the center of a web of trails. A quarter of a mile away, the golf cart sat parked—showing him she could adapt to his world had multiple facets. The longer she waited, the louder the forest became: the scurrying of mice, the screeches of hawks, the buzzing of bees, the falling of seeds. Helios stood fast at the reins.

A branch snapped; she looked; there was nothing to see but she knew there would be. She measured her stillness by the rhythm of her breathing and blinked as little as possible. Another branch snapped and she ignored the itch on her face. It had been eight hours. The trigger was warm.

A patch of brown and white moved. There were rustling sounds along the ground when, as if magically sprung from the earth, a doe appeared, trailed by its fawn. The mother extended her neck to survey the area with all senses. A few moments of stillness passed before she and her offspring hurtled some bushes. The movements of the animals were mechanical yet fluid: limbs contracted with easy grace, heads floated like hummingbirds. Her cheek pressed against the stock of her rifle and through the scope she gauged they were fifty yards away.

In the kill zone patience was her forte. She had a knack for sensing the perfect shot and in this moment it seemed she had a choice of several. She panned the crosshairs over the doe's vital organs: a shot to the heart, a shot to the liver. *No, that would not do.* She did not forget there was a point to be made.

The deer took turns munching leaves and standing guard, heads popping up and down like the buttons of a chess clock. They were having their fill. Faith was ready. A shot at the top of the neck, in a target a square inch in size, would cripple the central nervous system and kill her instantly. *Rest after such a long trek*, she thought. The doe tilted her head and Faith held her breath. The shot cracked; the fawn bolted; the mother crumpled to a heap, dead in her tracks.

At precisely five o'clock she arrived behind La Maison—with hooves hanging stiffly from the side of the golf cart. A relieved Mann greeted her from the doorway, already bettered by realizations that made her actions less surprising. They butchered the deer together and talked about the hunt, and he marveled at her marksmanship to her satisfaction.

For dinner, they had venison.

"That was delicious," he groaned. "I can't believe it. I used to eat this all the time when I was a boy. I...I mean...it really must be ten years since I've eaten roasted deer."

She smiled with her eyes. Her confidence was growing.

"And your preparation," he added. "Simply perfect."

She leaned forward with arms folded. "What was that food you served at dinner when we met? The black slices on top of the soup?"

Mann gulped his water and wiped his mouth with the

back of his wrist. "Truffles."

"What are they?"

"They're a kind of fungus. Mushrooms that grow underground."

Her chin was so low it almost touched the table. "They smelled so good. And so *strong*."

"They're very fragrant. They were once considered a delicacy, served rarely. They were very expensive."

"Really?"

He nodded. "I think it was because they were difficult to farm. Not impossible, just expensive to maintain economically. And it can be a challenge to find them. They grow near oaks and sequoias. I once read about them in an encyclopedia and learned that people used to train dogs and pigs to search for them, so the first time I actually came across some I fed a couple to Marquis and he loved them, and when I was feeding them to him I said *Truffles! Truffles!* over and over again," he laughed, "and so the next day I came back and yelled *Truffles!* and he comes trotting over, so I took him out on a truffle hunt and he found some more in about twenty minutes."

Faith chuckled. "Who's Marquis?"

He quieted. "He was a pig I had."

"Oh." She paused. "Well, I think truffles are delicious."

He sighed silently. "If I'd known you would be so fond of truffles, maybe I wouldn't have served pork shoulder at the banquet."

She raised her eyebrows.

"But I have some more in the kitchen. Maybe tomorrow I'll make that soup again for you."

"That would be wonderful." They shared some silence. "Isn't the whole concept of culinary delicacy funny?"

"It is," he answered. "It's ironic that only the rich could afford fungus."

"Or shark fin," she interjected.

"Or sea urchin," he added.

She wrinkled her nose. They laughed like friends having an inside joke. Then the laughter faded, and she sensed the perfect shot.

"So what are you doing tomorrow?"

He stopped moving and exhaled. "I have to feed the livestock, dig soil, and pick apples. I also saw a wet patch outside the house, at the base at the corner where Paine's bathroom is. I'll have to check to see if there's something wrong with his plumbing."

"That reminds me. When you showed me around La Maison, you didn't indicate that Joy had quarters."

"That's because she doesn't have any. Joy is always gone. She only comes to me to share a vision she's decided I need to be aware of."

"Oh." She waited.

He spoke. "Do you want to help me compost tomorrow?"

She beamed. "Yes. And pick apples...?"

"Everything," he assured.

"I would like to very much."

"Good. We'll be up early again." He stood and they cleared the table.

The two went upstairs, exchanged good wishes and parted gleeful and expectant. She was committed to working hard: farm labor was a childhood memory. Her affection for him was taking on complexity, and the lessons were mounting.

Love was more than to be felt. It was something to be exposed to, something to be learned.

An hour later, he was staring at the ceiling, *Robinson Crusoe* spread on his chest: she was sitting up, propped by half a dozen pillows, when she turned the middle page of *Romeo and Juliet*.

The Lost Men

* *

The next day Mann was amazed at how quickly chores were finished with Faith's help. He was a bit stronger but she was a bit faster and the tasks' completion took half the time. Their efficiency allowed for more frequent rests, and several times he found himself staring at her neck.

The details of her form mesmerized him. Glances were all he would dare when they were silent. The sharp edge of where her skin met her lips was a feature he kept returning to, as was the subtle concavity spread across the face of her hips.

Afternoon hikes became a routine for the two. The days accumulated into weeks, and change was abundant. On one such walk Faith discovered a cave that led to an underground brook, providing a new water supply that was probably much cleaner. Every pair of drapes in La Maison was tied open, and there were no truffles left in the kitchen.

The shortened workday led to more than wilderness excursions. Sometimes they would drive and explore, search neighboring homes for entertaining possessions, play music, play games, or simply talk. She had never felt this patient. Laughter had grown into a loyal companion.

One day, after a late lunch, they retired to the library.

"Do we have any video material here in La Maison?"

He replied, "D'you mean like DVD or VHS?"

"Yes."

"No," he answered. "It wasn't really designed to last."

Sprawled on the window seat, she put her hands over her eyes. "That really would be something to see, wouldn't it? A video recording of people?"

"It would," he said. "A prized possession."

She swiveled her body and sat up. "D'you even *have* a prized possession?"

"You mean *a* single prized possession?"
"Yes."
His knee began to bounce. He was looking out of the side of his eyes and thought a moment longer.
"Well...I think there are two answers to that."
She perked up. He had learned how to manipulate her body by being coy or playful. It was almost puppetry.
"No, you *have* to choose one," she demanded.
He stood. "I'll show you."
They left the library together. She badgered him with immature insistence, exaggerating the importance of a prized possession to be a one-and-only item.
He entered the study first, the two still humming with delight.
"*Let me guess*," she blurted. "The Hrabanus Maurus folio?"
"No," he replied as he walked to his desk.
"Okay." She paced in the opposite direction. "The bust of Ezra Pound?"
"*No*."
She turned. "I give up."
He sat behind the desk. She came over. He opened a drawer.
"Of the art in this house, you're right: the folio and the bust probably are my two favorites. But there's one thing I have that I would say is more *meaningful* to me than any other."
She was captivated.
He reached into the open drawer and pulled out a small chalkboard.
"*What is that?*" she asked in a hoarse whisper.
He turned the slate around and placed it on the desk in front of her. It had drawn on it, in white chalk, a grid of boxes and a bit of writing. As she looked closer the signs registered.

The Lost Men

"It's a calendar." He nodded with a curious smile.

The warmth of discovery spread through her face.

"Today is June the 6th, 2206."

She grinned and looked up. *"It is?"*

He shrugged. "It is."

She looked back down at the board. His penmanship was intriguing.

"D'you know your birth date?"

"No," she answered.

"Well why don't we make it today? We can celebrate tonight with a special dinner...and lots of wine."

She laughed. "Okay!"

"Really?" he said. "I'm being serious...are *you?*"

"Yes!"

"Your first birthday party...?"

She laughed uncontrollably. *"Yes!"*

"Great. Perfect. June 6. From now on." He smiled broadly. "Starting tonight."

She was blissful. Both were fidgety.

He took the calendar back and closed the drawer.

"So what is the other one?"

"The other what?"

"Your *other* most prized possession."

He walked around to her side of the desk and sat on its edge. "Well, the other possibility is...that my prized possession is something I don't yet own."

She furrowed her brow.

He resumed. "Something timeless, something beautiful..."

"Like what?" she asked quizzically.

He folded his arms. "Like a portrait of you."

The warmth of flattery spread through her chest.

"Would you come with me downstairs?" he asked.

She could not remember if she said yes.

David A. Colón

*   *

When posing she became more serious. He sat her in an embroidered throne, folded her hands, tilted her chin. He stood and knelt and stood as he circled, primping folds and meting out directions. Every detail of the image was choreographed to perfection before he took to his vantage at the easel.

He walked away, picked up a charcoal, and turned. Gazing upon her felt surreal; it was as if he was already staring into a work of art. They seemed nervous, each wanting to please the other, and both could not help but feel undeserving. Self-consciousness denied her access to his thoughts.

"Now if you can, try to relax."

"I will."

They would never remember the experience as unfolding in time. From the first glittering scrape until the moment she stood, emotions welled from their spewing hearts, enough to lose themselves completely. With a small fan brush he molded depth onto the form. If she were not so beautiful, he might have taken liberties: pointillism, cubism. But anything less than a natural depiction would have been a sin. He added details with an ivory toothpick, counting the eyelashes to manifest her symmetry. It was clear he believed that love must be honest, that hopes had no place in finding its root, that one must not project oneself, that he must love her for who she is.

The color of the sky had changed when Mann ended the session.

"I think that'll be all for today. You must feel stiff."

She relaxed into the chair. "Really?"

He froze. *"No?"*

She crossed her legs. "Actually, yes. Not really *stiff*, though." She made eyes at him.

The Lost Men

He cracked his knuckles and stood before her. "It's taking shape. I hope you'll like it."

She leaned forward. "I'm sure I'll treasure it."

"Well, I think I'll get in the kitchen and begin your birthday dinner." He had energy, and almost started to leave.

"*Wait*," she said. "There's no hurry."

Still smiling, he turned back. "You're right."

Her crossed leg bounced gently.

"Will you sit for me tomorrow?"

In the pause, she stood, walked up and whispered into his neck:

"I'll *lay* for you *tonight*."

He felt weak, chilled with warmth. Their breaths touched. Their hands touched. Clothes fell to the floor piece by piece. In the twilight their bodies mingled. The slow kiss grew deeper, the furniture moved. Their passion was everywhere to be seen: on his naked back, in her skyward feet.

Nine

Every day, of the months that followed, they made love. They acted naturally. Their daydreams were trembling, slick, pungent.

She slept in his bed. He read much less. One night, in the wee hours, Paine moved his belongings into Faith's quarters, the whole time chuckling over the idiom, "to shoot the moon."

The day's labor was always swift; lunch was a doorway to diversion. The counsels were more of a presence—cleaning, gardening—and in time the couple explored more of the region. One night, between pillows, Mann told Faith about the Palace of Fine Arts, and she made him promise to take her there.

They drove as far as the edge of Golden Gate Park and walked. They shared stories, asked questions, flirted and kissed in the afternoon sun. With her encouragement he untied a pedal skiff from a tourist station on the reservoir, helped her in and pushed off for them to coast around the slimy pond. Later they came upon the Tea Garden.

Under a moss-covered pagoda, and in his arms, she said, "Fate has been kind."

"Yes it has."

"So much so that I wonder if we have enough."

He pulled his head from her. "Enough of *what?*"

"Enough of fate."

"Enough of fate?"

"Yes. Enough of fate." She kissed him. "Enough fate so as to make our own."

He repressed an urge to push her away.

"Don't you feel how strong we are together?" she asked.

"Of course I do."

"*Must* we succumb to fate any longer?" she asked suddenly. "Why are Paine and Joy still with us? Mann, what more could fate do for us?"

With this, he let her go.

"No, come back," she pleaded. "I mean this for you. I mean this for *us*. I love you, Mann, and I love nothing else."

"And I you."

"And this is all I need to see. I don't need Paine or Joy to tell me what's to come. I *have* you; we're together; we'll bear our seed and raise a child and be a family and live, and weather life together." She let his arm go.

"You're right," he said. "We will do all those things. But the counsels will relieve themselves when it is fate to do so."

"But if we send them off," she implored, "then wouldn't it mean that it was *fate* for us to send them off?"

"You're being nefarious."

"*How so?* You think my little words can offend fate?"

He looked at her sternly.

"Mann, I'm serious." She paused. "How do you know that fate isn't speaking to *me*, telling *me* to convince you of the power of *your* will?"

His anger subsided.

"There, you see?" she asked. "We know what we want to do and what we need to do. We can fend for ourselves," she suggested as she came closer, "and be safe."

He accepted her embrace. They leaned against the wall.

She said, "Who needs them? To tell us what tomorrow

will bring? To say the sun will rise? To foresee a mare in foal? We *already* do that. We see the future, too, every day. We know when the chickens will be fed, and they will; we know that rabbit will be eaten, and it will. Tonight we'll make love, we'll sleep until dawn, we'll cook, we'll read, we'll love. We see the future and we make the future. It's one and the same; we make our *own*. It couldn't be any other way. Think about it: how could you have survived the seven years of your solitude without seeing into the future?"

He thought.

"Could you not predict the seasons? Didn't you rotate crops? Didn't you foresee the need for a pigsty, and build it, and make it real? Didn't you ever predict rain, and be right? Even the most minute things: I mean, don't you even just feel an itch, and in doing so know, absolutely *know*, that in but a second or two you are going to scratch it and make it go away? And it happens? Is *that* not seeing into the future? If you think about it, isn't *every* action, every human action, every mindful, thoughtful, willful action, predicated wholly and directly upon seeing into the future?"

His pause was a tacit agreement.

"And you? Haven't you always known what you *wanted?*"

He admitted as much.

"*And hasn't it come true?*"

"Yes it has."

Her tears broke. "So has it for me."

They hugged tighter. She put her lips to his ear and whispered:

"*You own fate.*"

He listened but committed to nothing.

With one hand on the pagoda the two stood on three legs, and he entered her.

The Lost Men

*   *

That evening Joy approached Mann for the first time since the one had come. They sat in the parlor.

"The Palace of Fine Arts was glorious," he gushed. "The sky was very clear. It was beautiful."

She clasped her hands demurely. "Was she impressed?"

"Yes she was."

"And how is she?"

"Wonderful." His adoration beamed.

"I was troubled when you were gone."

The warmth of fear spread through his face. "Why?"

She shook her head. "I don't know."

She had nothing to say. She just needed to see it for herself.

That night the bathtub faucet did not work. By the time Mann finished fixing it, Faith had been asleep for hours.

*   *

The trip to Golden Gate Park and the Palace of Fine Arts was so enjoyable that the two took another the next day. This time they drove up Highway 101 to the Embarcadero. On the right the piers appeared; on the left, the ruins of San Francisco.

The seaside stench was putrid. A cove of rocks between two docks was trimmed with more than a hundred seals, basking and writhing in fat, helpless forms like an orgy of slugs. Barks and grunts shot through the air from the nest as it murmured with growls and belches. Seagulls hovered over the beached pod, scavenging morsels of who knows what.

It was obvious that the restaurants and shops had been destroyed by fire. But both piers were intact, many boats still docked. They walked out to the marina, studied their surroundings, and after discussing options decided to kayak. The two strapped on life vests and agreed that Mann should stroke, then cut into the first waves and caught the flow of the bay.

After a spell the silence broke with a yell and they spoke strategically to coordinate their efforts to reach the island's shore. The kayak ran aground smoothly, carving water into the sliding sand.

The prison stood like a fortress, though the skeletal ruins of annexes looked leprous and moldy. Neither knew what the graffiti about "Indian Land" really meant, nor that its lettering had been preserved and restored by curators. They ascended a wide, zigzagging path to the mouth of Alcatraz.

"In this prison they kept only the worst criminals," he said with morbid interest. "Killers, rapists...all manner of sociopaths."

She thought deeply. "It seems so unjust: to suffer the burden of caring for lost men."

He disagreed.

"Why not?" she asked.

"I think housing killers in a penal colony like this, though on moral grounds unjust, was one of the more prescient measures society took."

She squinted. "You're being contradictory."

"You know I object to the penal system, but nevertheless the belief that lost men were incorrigible and needed to be extricated from society showed foresight."

"But weren't killers kept in prisons like this to be rehabilitated?"

"Only in theory, and not until the nineteenth century. A prison sentence for murder was a lifetime."

"So why did they keep them alive?"

He did not know.

"It seems so incongruous." She spoke with her hands.

The Lost Men

"It seems society knew that lost men were *born* lost because they imprisoned them for life, but it also seems society did *not* know that lost men were born lost because they nurtured them."

"And some actually *were* freed," he noted.

They passed through darkness before the space was lit by giant gated windows. Placards stood on easels for tourists, denoting prison narratives wavering between ambivalence and sympathy.

"Did you know that the day Joy told me you were to come, a lost man shot down my pesticide plane?"

She looked at him with round eyes. "*What?!*"

He nodded.

She was dumbfounded.

"He died. Joy cremated him."

"Did you see him?"

"No."

She looked worried. "I've never seen a lost man before...nor had my parents, nor Paine."

"Neither have I. That was the closest I ever came to a lost man."

She crossed her arms. "For so long I've hoped that lost men no longer lived."

"Well, believe me, they do. They're born naturally, and fate finds ways to protect them."

"How?" she asked. "*Why?*"

They leafed through insensible explanations but agreed that the modern-day killer was of a different breed.

The two-story hallway was lined with barred cells: caustic chambers scarred by the ragged spots of peeling paint. At one end they came to a doorway that led to two turnstiles. The wall was covered with hooks from which hung a hundred headsets. They spent ten minutes switching every single plug, trying to find a working combination of the right headphones and audio media.

David A. Colón

Nothing connected.

"Bank robbery seemed big, too," she said. "That one over there said a man spent twenty years here for it."

He smirked. *It was the Age of Money.*

"And did you see the bootlegger?" she asked excitedly.

"Yes: Al Capone?"

"The one from Chicago?"

"Yes."

"From the 1920s?"

"Yes."

She glanced down. Her foot swiped at the silt. She paused for effect, then asked, "*Any relation?*"

He looked at her like a cat at a mouse. Their exchange of panicky smiles launched the ensuing chase. Her shrieks of laughter echoed. After a spurt of quick, heavy footsteps at the corridor's end, he caught her by the waist and wrestled her into a corner cell. Some moments of faint rustling preceded a whining moan, rising to unbridled wails as they pounded hips on the woolen cot.

*   *

They stayed long enough to see everything on the island before making the trip home. When they arrived at La Maison, the counsels surprised them with a barbeque supper. The four dined together for the second time. They ate and drank for hours.

After showering they took to different activities; she wove a basket, he played guitar. Like the scattered sheets of music atop the piano, his thoughts were distracting. One last chord strummed and the instrument was put down. He imagined the room without its stands and cases; for a long time he had known this someday would be quarters. Building a bed, painting a mural: fantasies orbited his image of the child. He wondered if they would have a son or a daughter, for he believed, mistakenly, that his affections would differ by gender. A boy would need constant discipline, and should be subjected to danger at an early age. *But a girl*, he thought: a girl he could coddle, a girl he could hug, a girl he could kiss. He paced around. He looked out the window.

Faith almost entered the room but stopped outside the doorway to watch him in silence. She saw him stoop, with his arms spread in front of him, and mime the action of catching a running child, and he lifted and hugged the invisible toddler and walked with a bounce as he stroked its head. The rapture of fatherly love possessed him. He was unaware of the spy.

She felt happy, disappointed, and jealous. He would make a good father but this display smacked of weakness, and dividing his affections between her and the unborn was getting ahead of himself. The effect ran her emotions cold. It dawned on her that his mannerisms were ancient, which tipped the balance back to a feeling of satisfaction, and she grinned stiffly.

He was cradling the dream in his arms when she entered.

"There you are," she said.

"Oh!" He turned with a start and dropped his hands to his sides. "You startled me."

"I'm sorry. What were you doing?"

"I was reading some Mozart...just absorbing the score. You know how I gesture when I take in music." He chuckled.

"Oh."

She had come to the room with the intent of initiating sex, but after an exchange of superficial jokes, she went back downstairs.

*   *

The next day, in the afternoon, she coaxed him into another trip. He preferred to rest and read, so they compromised on a modest excursion to Stanford. For the drive he chose the Jaguar.

They turned off El Camino Real onto Palm Drive, a dead-straight path into the university. Bushes bulged to wild heights, walling in the road. Towering palms and eucalyptus trees swayed in the distance. Like a pot of gold, the fresco on Memorial Church was a faint mirage.

They came to an oval patch of land at least an acre in size. The roundabout led to the red-painted curb where they parked.

"The architecture looks just like La Maison," she remarked.

"Spanish Mission."

They climbed the steps to the Main Quad.

"That's called Hoover Tower," he pointed. "It's quite a view."

"Can we go to the top?"

"Sure."

"Have you ever been to the top of it?"

"Mm hmm. You can even see La Maison."

She smiled like a child.

In an open lawn they came to a cluster of statues: wretched, disproportionate figures. The stone plaque identified them as Auguste Rodin's *Burghers of Calais*. She touched their massive hands, examining the upward bend of their fingernails. He looked into their gouged eyes. Their sockets were tattered, expressions locked in the patience of blindness.

The Main Quad was paved with hexagonal bricks. Cherry blossoms on stone pedestals stood in bloom like snow-covered mountains. They talked about the chipped painting on the face of Memorial Church.

Inside was darkly lit by the rainbow light of stained

glass. Their footsteps echoed. After ambling through the nave she perched herself in the mahogany pulpit.

He called to her. "I want to show you the organ."

Wooden stairs led to the balcony. She took in the view from the edge as he sat at the keyboard. The restoration of this pipe organ, to which he came on occasion, to play, took years. Priming the instrument for this very moment was one of the chores he completed in the three days before she arrived.

The church vibrated with a medieval hum that weighed her down into the pew. He played a piece, by an Italian missionary, called The Ascension. The final chord held for many seconds, and when it ended their hearts expanded into the silence. It was the most intense and uplifting musical experience she had ever had. Her praise became flirtatious. He entered their embrace innocently, though it evolved into love-making.

*   *

The next building was Green Library. Large windows lit the lobby.

"Okay, let's play a game," he said. "Let's go our separate ways and search the stacks and see which one book each of us comes up with. In ten minutes."

She was open to the challenge. "Okay, but ten minutes is so short."

"Well, how long then?"

"How about an hour?"

"*An hour?* No...say, twenty minutes."

She tilted her head. "Why so short?"

"Come on," he said spiritedly, "this is just a game! We'll find more books later."

She gave in. "Okay." They wound their watches.

"Okay," he said. "Now...go!"

David A. Colón

He strode quickly; she took barely a few steps. Beyond the lobby was dark. A wide, carpeted staircase led her up to the second floor, which was even darker. The aisles smelled of brittle paper. In only one direction was there a window. She walked close to the books, trying to distinguish their titles, but it was useless, so she returned downstairs.

The loan desk extended into the lobby. She leapt, between two computer screens, onto and over the counter. The employee side revealed cubbies stocked with index cards, pencils, and staplers.

Her jump knocked open a main drawer. Inside was a row of stamps: chrome with black handles, like gourmet corkscrews. She pulled out the largest one. The rubber underside was stained by layers of red and green ink. She sucked her tongue before spitting a small mist at the tip. On a pad of paper she pounded the stamp with force; the spring mechanism punched and released. The faint imprint read "JAN 6 2013."

Behind her was an island of shelves holding books of every size and design. Each volume stood with a turquoise marker tucked in its pages. The sign read "Reserves."

Outside in the autumn wind, Mann swaggered with a black book under his arm. What he had had in mind was in a display at the Hoover Archives.

After nineteen minutes, they reconvened.

"What'd you get?" he asked in an outdoor voice.

She leapt over the loan desk. "This book by Gordon Brotherston, *The Cayman's Lexicon*. It's very interesting; it deciphers the hieroglyphics of Mesoamerican codices."

His own interest surprised him. "Really?"

She handed him the book, holding the pages with pictures open.

"So what did *you* find?"

He changed directions instantly. "A first edition of the

London publication of Marx and Engels' *Communist Manifesto*."

"*Wow*," she said. "Let me see that."

"Look. It doesn't say anywhere that it's a first edition, but there's one discernible feature that ensures its authenticity." He turned to the back, found the letter and pinched his fingertip to the page. "There's an umlaut missing here, where it says 'workers unite.'"

She looked closely. "Well done."

He gloated, still lost in pursuit of his moment stolen from the music room. The confusion of pride made a hollow victory in an unfair contest gratifying. She succumbed without effort and the two were happy in their very different thoughts. Together they searched for more books and left the library with weighted knapsacks.

She shielded her eyes in the evening sun. The walk to Hoover Tower featured a totem park and a moss-covered fountain. After panting up dozens of flights of stairs they reached the observation deck. A welcome breeze blew through the spacious, caged vista. Beyond the grille the miniature world was a tranquil panorama. As always, excitement led to comfort; witness turned to words. In her uterus, cell division was moving through its paces, and it was uncertain as to where the child was conceived.

Ten

The signs came gradually. The first was menstrual. *Pregnancy, perhaps*. But conjecture revealed mortifying alternatives, so they remained uncertain.

The next, after two months, was nausea. In the middle of every night, under fluorescent light, he would find her kneeling weakly on the bathroom tiles. But again hopes cowered; *it could also be a virus*. For a long time the fact of conception skulked with grave uncertainty. Hence, once they were sure, there was no celebration except private joys.

Their faith grew, as did she. Her work was restricted to household duties, though an afternoon fright—she found a pile of rat feces in the pantry—curtailed these chores as well. Noon and night Mann pampered her with the discretion of a butler. It proved Napoleon, too, had a snout for truffles.

The counsels said nothing. They forecast nothing, and their demeanor showed that this was to be taken as a natural course. Mann was disappointed with them, for they never seemed to have visions anymore, and increasingly would return to the conversation he had with Faith under the pagoda.

Because of the shortened winter days, it was dark by the time he would come home from work. She would be soundly dreaming in her evening nap; her sleep pattern had

The Lost Men

been halved. A stainless steel pot bubbled with elk heart and dandelions. She was sick of cornmeal and eggs. Her favorite foods required hunting.

Mann sat in the salon, listening to Marvin Gaye, leafing through a crate of records newly procured from Stanford's Archive of Recorded Sound. On the table, a crystal filled with sangria, ice, and fermented fruit stood in a pool of condensation. He had become reacquainted with solitude. The only time they spent together anymore was an hour at lunch and an hour before bed. And this made him happy. He had his woman; he had time to think; he was alone yet surrounded. The future was perfect. Faith was as beautiful as ever, and her burden was to be respected in spite of symptoms.

The same song was replaying for the second time. He was anticipating the lyrics when the record skipped, then stopped.

The ice cubes tinkled. The ground trembled and the walls shuddered and the inlaid ceiling rattled. A tremor surged through La Maison like a pulse of electricity. In the kitchen, the scalding pot crashed and splashed under a billow of steam. It stopped. Glass quieted. A purple slice of orange lay on the wet carpet like a gasping goldfish.

He left the salon to go upstairs and check on Faith when something caught his eye. A shadow outside the dining room window passed through the moonlight. He opened the glass doors and walked out onto the deck. For a moment he heard the sound of claws scratching wood. Three raccoons scampered across a patch of lawn between two bushes. He lingered. Nothing else moved. He almost turned back when he saw the rest. A gang of nine more crossed the same patch of lawn. Their simian-like movements were unmistakable in the night.

To his right, alongside the shrubs, he had parked a pickup truck. Its bed was filled with rotten fruit, kitchen scraps, and peat meant for compost. The neatly packed mound had been torn into a mess. He remembered the pesticide plane; maybe letting it go was a mistake after all. *Faith*—he bounded up the stairs two at a time.

*   *

She did not like *The Yellow Wallpaper*; it was a disturbing read. Around ten o'clock she came outside wearing heavy gloves and holding a spade. It had occurred to her that cultivating a greater variety of herbs would be a good idea. And besides, these days her body felt restless. Oftentimes standing hunched in a half squat was the most comfortable position to be in. Ergo gardening.

She was wearing a new dress she had made. It was orange velvet with a yellow daisy print. Finding maternity dress patterns took Mann weeks of intense searching before hitting the mother lode in a store called Michael's. Paine's living room drapes were expended. The dress's bulging seams were asymmetrical. Mann found her sloppiness endearing.

He arrived pushing a loaded wheelbarrow.

"Good morning," he chimed.

"Hello."

"You're up; d'you feel okay?" The question was obligatory.

"Yes, I feel better, thanks."

Better than what? he thought.

He set the wheelbarrow down. "D'you see these pumpkins?!"

She smiled and whispered a laugh. Her ponytail was coming undone.

"That's what a sty full of happy pigs looks like," he joked. "I'll save some for soup and pudding, and I'll also toast up the seeds. With salt and pepper, and some fennel seed, and some roasted walnuts," he imagined, "I bet you'd like that as a snack." He sounded hopeful.

She could not bear the thought of food. She stabbed at the soil like a maniac. *What is wrong with this thing? Why is it so dry underneath?* An ill-timed exhalation caused a sharp pain in her side. Her over-extended muscles cramped, and she staggered.

He helped her sit, inch by inch, and pulled off her gloves. Her crowded lungs fluttered like flightless wings. She panted and sighed for more than a minute.

"I've been thinking." She caught her breath. "About naming the baby."

He patted the pumpkin in his hands. "Oh?"

She nodded with an open mouth.

"Oh, well, let's hear some names."

"I don't have *lots* of them. I just have one particular one in mind."

Mann trod carefully. He turned over a large bucket and sat on it like a stool.

"Okay," he said softly.

"Boone."

"Boone?"

She nodded.

"Why?"

"It was where I was born," she replied. "I was born in a town called Boone."

"Boone," he repeated. "If it was where you were born, then it would be very meaningful...*Boone*...it has character."

She agreed. She knew before saying anything that this was going to be the child's name.

"I think Boone's a perfect name," he suggested. "I don't think I could find a better one."

Her contentment lasted about a second.

"I'm glad that was so clearly decided. I was going to..."

he began, but convulsed abruptly, and sank several inches. The rusted bottom of the bucket he sat on had caved in, his haunches wedged into the tin cylinder. His helpless look seeped into her before she wailed with laughter. He sucked through his clenched teeth before finding the humor in it, too, because he was still holding the pumpkin.

* *

Mann was jubilant; the portrait was finished. In the dusk light he dusted the canvas with a brush of feathery filaments. Her form glowed amidst soft oranges and pink, filled in every nook and curve. But if all one could see was just a sliver of her wrist, those eyes would know enough to say the artist loved her.

He left the studio. She was not in the billiards room. He called down the portico, then turned and traced his steps. In the den, Joy was sitting, in rigid posture, on the corner couch. They looked at each other but said nothing.

He entered the salon. Paine was standing. His elbow rested on the mantelpiece, under the painting of Lord Nelson. They exchanged a glance. Mann continued on through the kitchen and dining room. He was bursting with excitement about the portrait, but for now it was a private matter between him and his love.

He called her name a few times, even out of a window. He checked three rooms upstairs before hearing her faint response.

She was in the master bathroom. "Faith, I have a surprise for you," he boasted.

She stood holding the gathered hem of her dress in both hands.

"I'm ready," she said soberly.

He could hear the wetness of her bare footsteps. He was speechless. The toilet seat was beaded with water. Inside, sunk to the bottom, lay a small glob of blood, deep in color like a rose petal.

*   *

She decided to stay in the bathroom. The counsels huddled and lurked. Mann felt somewhere between and thus unsure of himself. He folded towels.

Faith paced. She held up the weight of her abdomen with her hands. Pacing helped. He offered her comforts, which she declined again and again. After a while everyone left her alone.

Her cheeks and neck were hot and moist. Hours' worth of seconds ticked away. The uterine muscles had begun contracting. Every third was almost too painful to bear.

It was impossible for her to think beyond the moment. She remembered nothing and dreamed of nothing. Thoughts blew about like fallen leaves in a gust of wind, the spent remains of a function no longer demanded.

His mind was in a prayer-like state. She hummed with the power of birth; he could feel it through the walls. The pitch of her moans had changed, turned into croaks, and they echoed. She waddled between episodes of hip thrusts as the mass was molding into its conical shape. Three words, *this is it*, rolled through his head like a mantra. He thought of a boy in his adolescence, triumphant, dignified, a master of life. *Boone would prove something*, he believed. He had hopes for the future and an inkling of humanity's survival. She reached into her legs. Deep inside the numbed opening she could feel the skin of its head, soft like a crocodile egg.

He and the counsels converged.

"Come into the bath," he mentioned.

She winced. "No."

They stood in abeyance.

David A. Colón

She pulled her frock over her head and threw it in a corner. The sight of her naked, venous bulge was appalling. She plodded out of the bathroom: her crack had widened. Hands first, she crawled onto their bed, and on all fours swiveled her hips. The contractions stopped and she was seized by another pain, an orgasm without pleasure. More muscles she had never felt before tightened. She rolled onto her back to see the three at the ready. By Faith's feet Joy revealed a pair of gardening shears from a white cloth wrap. Paine cupped a towel in his hands.

She howled.

The room was sucked into silence. Mann was overcome by thoughts and emotions, not ideas but hopes, the expectant father anticipating his role. He quivered under the weight, the wait, like Samson, readying his mind for any fate, good or cruel. A stillbirth, a moron, a savior: it was now his duty to live only for the result, to transfer his instincts for survival from this body to the next. If only it would breathe, be alive, begin to grow: *then I could die, it would be alright to die.*

The life inside me. There's a life inside me. These were the only words spoken in her mind. Only now could she feel enough space for vantage, to see the chrysalis, the dry waste that she had become. *The life inside me.* It was strong and new: not a mind but the potential for one, not a person but the potential for one, absent and, for this, not a void but everything—a mystery, sacred.

*   *

She felt the tear, despair and release. Everyone froze before the collective sigh.

Now there was another, the world one richer.

The Lost Men

*   *

Paine backed away and turned with the swaddled infant.

Never had Mann felt so human: a member of a race. Every cell in his body breathed a sigh of relief, and he felt twenty years older.

Joy cut the umbilical cord with the shears. She placed a metal bowl by Faith's thigh. Mann was curious, and felt compelled to come to the mother's side, and was in a daze, and entrusted Paine, who surreptitiously left with the baby.

He grabbed his wife's hand and wiped her brow.

"What is it? A boy or a girl?" she asked hoarsely.

Mann was unsure. "Where did Paine go?"

Joy seemed to be listening to something else.

"Mann," Faith said, "is there something wrong?"

"No—I don't know," he replied, looking out the bedroom door.

"Because I feel like something's wrong." She tried in vain to shift her limp body. "I can't feel anything."

"It's a boy," Joy said.

"A son?" he asked. *Boone will be a great man.*

"Did you hear me? I said I can't feel anything."

Mann came to. Joy went after Paine.

*   *

He spent a year-long day by her side. Everyone was gone and he would not leave her alone. She complained of the pains that suddenly left her paralyzed, and had not moved an inch since the child left her.

Mann was confused; he had anticipated nearly everything but this. His reflex was to bond with mother and child in a family embrace, and, in its absence, he stood vigil restlessly.

The child was gone. Faith's discomfort was worsening

and she was having trouble describing it. He had not yet even touched his son. Her body had begun to slouch, vegetative. He had urges to leave and take the child back from them. She looked pale and clammy; her eyes had darkened. *A temporary complication. It has to be. It has to be.*

He brought his face close to hers. "I'm going to find them and bring Boone here to you. I'll be right back."

"No, don't leave me!" she begged.

"I'll be right back," he assured.

The situation tested two instincts. One gave in to the other, and he stormed out.

Down the hallway, at the top of the double staircase, he was met by Joy.

"Come no further," she commanded, tall, hand raised.

"What?!" he objected, unfamiliar with this tone of hers.

Paine appeared halfway down one side of the stairs. He cradled the baby, a tiny swathed bundle of white.

"Give him to me now!" Mann shouted.

Joy's hand was still up. "No," she said. "He is no longer your child."

"He never was," Paine added.

"Give him to me now!"

"Mann," Joy began, "We have seen the child's fate."

"No you have not!" he yelled. "He is my son, *our* son, and we will take him from you and you will leave us alone as a family!"

"That will not happen," Paine said.

"It is you who will leave," Joy added.

"*What?!*"

"We have seen its fate," Paine responded. "It is undeniable."

The counsels looked at each other.

Mann saw the certitude in their glance. They knew this to be true; he was sure of their conviction.

The Lost Men

It took a few moments more for him to accept. If Boone was not to be theirs, was not to be trusted to join them and live and be nurtured, if he was not their son, then it could only mean one thing, a prospect Mann had always known. His throat and eyes grew hot with tears.

"*Wait*," he gasped.

In the bedroom, Faith lay like a corpse.

"Oh..." she moaned.

"I'm here." He sat by her side.

"Where is he?" she asked weakly. She noticed his welling eyes. "What is it?"

He trembled in composure. "Everything's wrong," he said.

She waited.

He held her hand in his. "They're sure."

To whisper was a labor. "Sure of what?" she asked.

He had no strength to say it. The room was thick with silence, like a sea wreckage.

It confirmed her worst fear, the one she had spent her whole life hiding.

*   *

She sighed.

She closed her eyes.

A stream of tears rolled down from each corner, into her ears.

"I'm sorry," she whispered.

"For what?"

"For what we've lost."

"*Don't say it.*"

"How can this be?" she asked herself. This was not supposed to happen; pains were taken by all to keep this possibility unspoken.

He said, "I love you. We have each other."

David A. Colón

Her ill face looked young. Breathing was becoming difficult. He had never felt so powerless. He squeezed her hand, held it to his mouth, kissed it, and asked, "Can you feel that?"

Her nostrils flared. She breathed.

He folded her arm onto her breast. He moved some of the hair draped around her neck and kissed her chest.

"Can you feel that?" he asked again.

She said she could not.

He came closer, looked down into her eyes. It told of his adoration. His head lowered and he kissed her lips. The instant hushed: he spoke a life in the span of a touch. He pulled from the kiss. The release could be heard.

"Did you feel *that?*" he asked quietly.

She made no breath. Her mouth held open as she swallowed with effort. Tears glistened on her eyes and teeth, and she whispered without a voice:

"*No.*"

*   *

He exhaled, and the crying came. He was wracked by the guilt of his imperfections; she deserved better; *can there really be no more giving?* He rested his head on her heart and sobbed. His eyes squeezed shut. The pain of loss ravaged him. His face gushed, and he wailed, the one utterance as old as humankind.

The tears poured, flushing his eyes of witness, a sprung leak of memories. Happy days and pleasures surged away like ocean fog. He remembered watching her sleep. The feelings grew acerbic. The tears were sharp and dry. His eyes stung, knotting, hurting more and more.

He let her body go and shrank from the bed. Still shaking, he wiped his cheeks with his knuckles. He tried to look, but the lids would not open. He touched his face with his hands. There was nothing to feel behind the skin and lashes. His eyes were flat, and sealed shut.

The counsels entered.

He heard them, and turned, rabid:

"*Look at what happened to me!*"

In his blindness they could show their fear.

"You must leave now," Joy said.

"You!" he shouted. "*You* leave! You wretches! You *demons!* You who live on the hopes of others, and pick at us like vultures! How can you bear yourselves?! You knew, all this time, didn't you? You had your visions, you saw the fate of this, you knew it to be an evil child, that it was a monster, that it would kill us! You *slaves* of this fate, this fate that bleeds death from a kinder heart! The fate that rewards the righteous with silence and murder!"

The two cringed.

"*To hell with you!*"

Paine shielded the baby.

"*This is fate's sentence?!*" he demanded, and pounded his chest. "For *me*, life's loyal subject, for all I've done to stem the tide and hang from hopes for lives I'll never know, or who will never know of me?!"

He seethed. The air boiled with his screaming hate.

"And *you!!*" he shouted louder, meant for his counsel. "You *Judas!* How could you betray me so?! Weren't our hopes one? Did you not *feel* my filial love? Were you not there?!"

He staggered. They stood defensively.

"*How could you not intervene?!* How could you allow fate to command you to betray your charge? How was this the perfect way? What about *you?*"

They had had enough. This *was* an intervention.

"The child is lost. We know this to be true. You need know no more of this fate."

Joy said, with choked emotion, "It is time for you to

leave now."

Mann turned his back to them, facing the sediments of Faith. "*I will make my own fate*," he murmured.

In his mind he saw a desert.

The experience of leaving hurtled intervals of time. There was the scene of the deck, with no one in front of him; he recalled the image from its smell and sound. There was a darker space, with rows of empty cages, the rabbits having been eaten mouth to tail by rats. The powers of prevision were adapting to him. There was a waterfall. He could feel he was much further away.

Eleven

"No."

* *

He exhaled, and the crying came. He was wracked by the guilt of his imperfections; she deserved better; *can there really be no more giving?* He rested his head on her heart and sobbed. His eyes squeezed shut. The pain of loss ravaged him. His face gushed, and he wailed, the one utterance as old as humankind.

The noise receded. Her eyes closed; she could not feel him wither. Her mind drifted through memories and dreams, and she knew she would forever be exiled from reality. She was trapped in torment, a nightmare, a feeling of pure dread, without vision, claustrophobic, restrained by infinity.

Time moved at a different pace. The world fell from her, as did her body, shed like a reptile. Her mind was detached from any material form. It existed nowhere.

Thoughts gathered in wells between waves of mood. Eventually, they turned into words. She thought of all the things she wished she could have told Mann, feelings and hopes she had inside, the rest of the sentence the two had begun. *Why did he love me?* She wanted to know what lined his motives. She could feel him but he was not there,

The Lost Men

like an amputee.

And was I prideful? She pondered fate, though poorly understood it. She thought in terms of sin, absolution, guilt. Her mind was molded to the scales of cause and effect—there must be a reason for her tragedy. There must be a reason why she was still thinking, still awake in this no-place, trailing behind the fading footprints of her life without leaving new ones.

Of all the lives she had envisioned to prepare for survival, this was not one of them.

She had imagined a moment well into the future. Old, they stood at the edge of a cliff a mile above a forest of flowers. The glowing sun set on a day fit to be the last. Between them trickled a stream that thundered down into a rushing waterfall. The mist below was magnetic and cool. They held each other's hands yet somehow faced apart. The sunlight was very white. Birds sailed in the distance. Neither meant nor rued, they fell, together, down, twirling, into the abyss.

She had imagined a goodbye, as mother and father. Their son was grown: a man, tall and strong and gentle in form, a man in whom the light of prosperity shone, a guardian, one it was an honor to know. The farewell was as brief as their trust was firm. But he would cry. He loved them, and the tears he stooped to dry on her neck were cold and clear.

She had imagined mothering a child, a girl without a name. Busy in knee-high activity, the girl ignored her. The daughter changed form and age over and over before her eyes.

She spoke. "Do you see what you want?"

The girl did not respond.

"Do you know what you need? Will you swear to accomplish something? Will you promise to endure suffering? Won't you allow discretion to silence discord?

David A. Colón

If threatened, will you exercise any measure to survive? Do you know how to pretend to anticipate disappointment? Have you ever deceived yourself? Do you believe that reality is a collage of desires? Have you ever wondered why we have different words for present and future?"

The girl finally looked up.

"Yes," she answered.

This image held her mind. *Perhaps pride was not my sin.* What she had never done in her life, which she understood only now, was teach. Inadvertence notwithstanding, she had never imparted wisdom upon anyone. She never meant to or tried to. *The meaning of life is to remember to find joy in providing for others.* Experience was not meant for the self; the self dies. Life only happens in lessons learned.

She had imagined other men. They were of varied builds and shades, ones with different personalities, serfs of different lands. She bore a child with each, and fell in love with each, and watched each die, and grew old with each, and every permutation of the possibilities of fate she had mapped and traced onto each scenario. The sheer number of imagined lives rendered every one impractical. The chances of any one panning out diminished with the steady accumulation of more and more.

She had imagined being alone. She had never met the one, for there was no one to meet, and was content and whole. There was her and the world. This vision was the purest fantasy. It required a suspension of disbelief. *No one is whole; that is why we live.* This dream was the first she had after entering her solitude. The memory lay dormant until now.

But this fate she had not envisioned. As somatic as her life was, for paralysis to usher her to death was cruel.

Or perhaps just.

As for pride, she found her means for repentance. Her

confession would be silence: to stop thinking, to stop inflating her dying self with squalling hopes that have no form to fill. She would not say she was sorry; her apology would be to not say anything. She accepted she was finished. There was nothing left of her in the world—except Mann. *Perhaps he would orchestrate the perfect lyric for my demise.* She wondered what would become of him.

*   *

It was morning and Joy was in the kitchen filling a basin with water. The kitchen faucets were the only ones that worked anymore. The foundation of La Maison had become a well. The flood measured a few feet from the ground floor, and crept like ivy.

She strained to move the lead-like basin to the counter. The white towels were placed in, wrung a few times, and left to soak. She matched the handles and carried the tub off, and waddled, hunched, with effort.

She stopped to rest five times before reaching the bedroom. There Faith lay. Her clothes had been changed; the sheets had been changed. Her comatose body was heavy and still and different, like an heirloom forced into the décor.

Joy rubbed her bruised palms. It had been more than a month, enough time to ponder everything. *The end this came to was unfortunate.* There was a pleasure she took in being the last one standing, yet overwhelmingly felt a sense of waste. She had emerged unscathed, *but for what?* She still had her mind, and her body, and lives' worth of experience. There was no student; she felt like stealing. Mann would die, she was sure. What disturbed her as much as anything was that she was convinced there were more people. She was sure there were more, many, many

David A. Colón

more, and she believed she could find them, even knew where they were. She had convinced herself.

The basin sat by the side of the bed under a ray of warm light. Faith had disappointed her; as an investment, she left her bankrupt. But given her life and duty, she had spent little emotion. She loved none of them, so losing them was discomfort, not pain.

Her thoughts were of trickery. She knew exactly how this was all going to end. Everything she did was a diversionary tactic to take her mind off what was certain. She had some awareness of this; there was no doubt she was possessed by hope. It was not that she hoped she was wrong, just that maybe fate would redirect itself and change.

She sat on the bed next to Faith. She held a small towel over her face: to wring water drop by drop into her gaping mouth. The throat, the lungs, the heart, the blood: only air moved through Faith anymore. This chore was the only one Joy had, and it consumed every hour of every day.

But something stopped her. She pulled her dripping fist back and plopped the balled towel down into the basin. She wiped her hands on her shirt and got closer, on one knee. Faith's lips were an ashy purple. Joy swept her fingertip around the mouth. It was dry and cold. Her finger touched the chin, and gently pushed the mouth shut. Quietly, as if to not wake her, Joy folded her hands on her chest.

*   *

The sunlight shone through La Maison at the same angle as before but from another direction. One by one the portals were shut: blinds drawn, drapes untied, windows locked. She spent more time in each room than was necessary to do this.

The Lost Men

The nostalgia was fading. The emotional residue of codependency was everywhere, but something she could walk around, a substance to avoid making contact with. What kept the place alive had left, unrequited, a final migration. A mammoth fallen through the ice—La Maison was now a fossil.

The house was dark. *Paine was right*. She wore the poncho her one once wove her, the garment she had slept in ever since. From the silent salon she could see the light let in from the main doorway. It was the only way into La Maison left open. She looked into the salon and saw the empty chair in the middle. She looked back to the doorway and could see the outdoors, gold and green. She foresaw this, too, this hollow gesture of choice. She also foresaw the decision to be made, and foresaw feeling the rigid fibers of repression tighten beneath her dermis.

The door would stay open; she neither left nor closed it. She walked into the salon, and from her pocket took a tiny box. She sat in the chair in the middle of the room. After a sigh, she muttered something.

The match landed at her feet.

A surge of fire cut across the rug like a torpedo. Its wake expanded. The blue flame spread over the ground like a tsunami. The drapes caught fire. The sprawl sped as it ascended. First the light, then the noise, then the heat. The blaze was ravenous. It darted through various paths, chasing away the hoards of vermin, and soon had the sound of crashing waves. It sunk into its host. Walls collapsed. Joy was unrecognizable. The handful of oily smudges on the Picasso: burned, blistered, bubbled. The portrait of Faith stood on its easel in the studio, a blade of grass on the rim of a volcano.

*   *

David A. Colón

There was a gray, salty marsh. Dark, damp sand caked the roots of leafless bushes. Bulging between them were boulders spotted with divots: dead coral. It was an arid seascape. A million years before and Paine would have witnessed whales birthing above his head.

The child was silent. Already a day old, it had made no noise at all. It did not hunger—so many signs were there. The mass hung around his neck and shoulder in a sling.

Fate is perfect. He returned to the years of his solitude, the happiest time of his life. When alone, one could never be right or wrong. There were no laws in loneliness, no ideals to precipitate guilt.

He was ready to push the rowboat into the water. He adjusted his clothing and the sling, faced the ocean and knelt. With a finger he scraped the clay sand, forming the strokes from left to right: *Paine*. Each line was finished with flair. His fingernail was packed with sand.

High steps splashed in the water. The little boat rocked as he climbed in. Before long he found a rhythm, and the natural movement of the sea. *Fate is perfect.* The memory of Charity was large but bland. The oars spanked the surface when not precisely placed. He did not want to think anymore. *That was it.* This must be a culmination. More words could render it otherwise.

It began to rain. Paine rowed the oars, his fists making circles. The beach was far away. He was happy the means to amends finally came to him. He rowed with vigor, soaked in the heavy downpour.

The coast was a thin, black line. The waves were bigger and slower. He let the handles go and pulled the sling to peek at the baby: soft, round, smooth, innocent. *Life is trust*.

There was a black chain coiled at his feet. He scooted forward and reached for the irons. First the left, then the right: he clasped the cuffs around his ankles with a pair of bolts. He heaved the anchor over the side and almost lost his balance. The chain unraveled layer by layer, the pile shrinking faster and faster. He tried desperately to think of nothing. To finally be right was what he had waited his whole life for, and now that he was, he wanted to stay empty. He hugged the child close to his chest. There was a splash, and the rowboat flipped upside down.

Twelve

With the loss of his eyes, Mann opened a third. In his mind he could still see, see the memories. Depending on the smell and the sound and how the ground felt beneath his feet and the breeze in his hair, he could approximate the image of the moment by superimposition of the past. Nothing was quite exact, but it was a reflex: and the more he prodded this veneer, the more it felt like the soft spots were ready to give way.

Why lose a sense? Does fate speak in metaphor? In exile, his anger turned to inquest. It seemed the loss of a sense in exchange for the sixth was a way of feeling death, a sample, a taste, perhaps another lesson to learn in this life. He was calmer now, and almost ready to address this growing sensation of gratitude. *Only with clairvoyance could we really survive in this condition.* Some layers of his ego were vacant. *It promises to empower.* He was in awe of fate, had a bodily knowledge of how many planes it existed on. He felt like moss. He felt like water. He felt skinned, stewed, digested.

His awareness was relocated a trice into the future. He knew everything that was going to happen a full, thoughtful moment before it came to pass. The wilderness swirled one step behind.

Oftentimes his mind was dark and empty. He marched steadily on. It grew cold. At night he slept in a cave, and

The Lost Men

shivered.

In the morning he was wakened. A stream of ants flowed over his ankle. Each speck inflicted deadly pain, and he scratched them off with panic. *How much control such tiny things have.* With his new power he could envision the surface of the ground slither. The more he perceived it, the greater it grew. Outside the cave, a river of insects flowed on the forest floor, ten feet across, either way as far as could be seen. A billion pin drops pelting the sod: the brown leaves crackled with the footsteps of ants.

His legs itched with the red spots of ticks. The sun was strong. He stumbled through the woods. His body moved with a purpose he was unaware of—prevision tossed him from one hand to the other. A house appeared. He was hungry. Eyes fused shut, he saw the name on the mailbox. Inside, nothing was where things were in La Maison. His hands rubbed the doorways. He found a knapsack and some gear to take with him.

*   *

He was thinner. His fingers and chin had a different shape. With a towel, he removed a pail from the fire, a bubbling pot of snails, lemons, and water.

*   *

For years he lived in a warehouse that stored a pine crate of shotgun ammunition. Wandering in the wild was a frightening existence. He could smell different trees and would pick their fruit before they ripened. With the pots he took from the house, he boiled any manner of root. Animals competed with him for sustenance, and on occasion would hint that he himself was a suitable meal. His skin was dotted with parasites. From the warehouse

David A. Colón

he would venture on hunts, and sometimes be successful; he had harnessed prevision. The warehouse had become his home, a haven in a fanged world. He fired rounds by the box, ate moose and beaver. His blindness was very real.

On the day he used the last of the shot, life left the building. It had been a trove of murder, a fortune spent in exchange for borrowing the most precious and fleeting of substances.

Much of his mind was missing. Or dormant.

*   *

He stood over a wide stream, straddling two protruding rocks. Between his knees he held a fishnet. He stood perfectly still; he had learned the importance of standing still. Last summer, in the stupor of blindness, he ran too close to a grizzly bear, and it batted his head between its paws, leaving him deaf in one ear.

He had learned the manners of the wild. *Never move with haste*. The river throbbed with the salmon run and he was not alone. A bear, perhaps the same one, was in her perch, aware of him. After a catch, he knelt, hiding the knife he needed to bring forth the meat. He ate it raw, crouched, quickly, ready to move.

A sycamore tree yielded fresh eagle eggs, though the distraught mother left more claw marks in his skull. His sanity was very narrow. In a roomy cave his pot boiled the speckled ovals. Some of his fingernails were missing; he had been scraping the earth for truffles. *Where's a pig when you need it?* He would not overcook the eggs, in spite of the spitting fits.

He remembered the meals he had made and the life that he had and his education. He licked his palms, smoothed down his hair, and scratched his groin. *Cogito ergo sum.*

The Lost Men

Cui servire est regnare. Veni, vidi, vici. Dulce et decorum est, Pro Patria Mori. With his father he memorized a good deal of the Iliad:

> Μῆνιν ἄειδε, θεά, Πηληϊάδεω Ἀχιλῆος
> οὐλομένην, ἣ μυρί Ἀχαιοῖς ἄλγε ἔθηκε,
> πολλάς δ' ἰφθίμους ψυχάς Ἄϊδι προίαψεν
> ἡρώων, αὐτούς δέ ἑλώρια τεῦχε κύνεσσιν
> οἰωνοῖσί τε πᾶσι...

He had forgotten what it all meant. Something about deadly Achilles and the dogs of war. His father told him that in Attic, it is not 'shut the door' but rather 'put the door to.' His face and teeth were smeared with egg. He stood and spat seven times, sat, then stood again and spat fourteen times more. *Is this what culture has come to?* In moments he was sane. More languages returned. Spanish, Cervantes, Unamuno. A book called *El reino de este mundo* in which a slave escapes bondage by turning into a bird and flying back home.

Faith. He had thought about her little; she was gone a thousand times over. But now he would remember, wondering if she had died. He did not know what to say to her. He remembered a poem.

From Sargasso to Saragossa. Prudentius, "Hymn for the Burial of the Dead." He recalled the Latin, with its metronomic prosody, and could recite a translation with ease:

> We are incompatible elements joined,
> mortal and immortal. They fuse
> in the heat of the Lord's forge. Mankind
> is fashioned thus. For a time it stays,
>
> but the weld, which cannot hold, gives way,
> for spirit yearns to rise to the sky

David A. Colón

while flesh, which is earth, is drawn to obey
gravity's stern decree. We die,

and our contrary portions come undone,
but God is good and even yet
will not abandon anyone
who is His servant. Bodies rot

in congenial mire, and in the grave
the spirit is trapped that, lighter, fights
to rise, assert itself, and live.
For a time, the universe hesitates,

but flesh feels a sudden warming. Then
those cold bones twitch and corpses sigh,
reanimated, and rise again,
borne by the heavenly breezes, to fly.

Which of us would not groom the plot
of our departed? The shrouds, the myrrh
that preserves their corpses, are these not
the pains we take because we are sure

that Jesus' power will raise them? Saint
Tobias' father, Tobit the good,
refuses to eat his supper, can't
think of food, and is troubled: he should

perform the rites for the dead. For this
heaven rewards him well. His prize
is the cure of his blindness. Suddenly his
sight is restored and he blinks his eyes,

stunned by the light. The lesson is clear.
The ills of this world prepare us for
the joys of the next. We ought not fear
death, which we know is heaven's door.

The Lost Men

This life is all decline and loss,
fading beauty, waning strength,
and wasting diseases, leaving us
piteous ruins, and yet at length

heaven shall make us whole, repair
our derelict frames, restore, improve,
and make us perfect everywhere.
Why do we mourn, then, those we love

with foolish lamentations? No,
no tears! What we bury here in the earth
is only the seed from which will grow
a fresh green plant. In this rebirth

we cannot doubt, for we believe
in heaven. We gaze down into a hole
in the gentle earth that we see receive
our dead, who issued, body and soul,

from the mouth of God. In faith and trust
we commit to Him who does not forget
His creatures these remains, that dust
the winds may scatter but God shall yet

revive and reassemble. We
will live again and breathe His breath.
Christ promised this eternity
to the thief on the cross, and we, in death,

shall lie in Abraham's bosom, sweet
with flowers' perfumes, as Lazarus does,
while Dives, the rich man, writhes in the heat
of hell, repenting what he was.

Help us, O Lord, to earn the right

David A. Colón

    to walk in that paradisiacal
    garden we come from, and consecrate
    us to Your service, each and all.

    Gather us from this exile, bring
    us home again, we pray You. Save
    us who, in a cemetery, sing
    and sprinkle flowers on this grave.

In another time and place, he would have cried. *Goodbye, Love*. One egg remained in the pot uneaten.

            *   *

When he walked, animals fled. He looked like a wraith, an emaciated ghoul, white as milk and jabbering imitations of language. His burning eyelids were sucked flush against their empty sockets. His fingertips were orange with blood from the itch of boils and sores. Over the span of three days, he scratched away the remains of his member, his manhood peeling off in scabby flakes.

  Pain had returned to blindness, and this revived his indignant mind. He cursed fate with the sounds he made, and asked what he thought were rhetorical questions.

  But fate responded. His mind was lit; he had a vision. From a skyward vantage he saw a river. He watched himself squat by a hanging tree on the riverbank, remove a knife from his pocket, and, in turns, cut away his eyelids, casting them upon the river, and they flowed down its twinkling surface, lashes up.

  The vision gave him purpose. He limped down the hill, flailing with tics, a wake of urgency and entitlement swirling behind him in the growing darkness. The next thing he sensed was a river; next, he squatted by a hanging tree on the riverbank, reached into his pocket, and clicked open his knife.

The Lost Men

The veil was lifted.

His mind breathed, freed. He was a lightning rod, a desperately sought ground for a charge of light—and when it hit, he was forever changed. The darkness was shed; prevision widened. Revealed was the sub-topos of the world, like the sea depths, like Atlantis. The trees were sculptures: hilltops, mausoleums. Crystal snowflakes floated like pollen, the mountains replaced by a glorious desert.

What do I see? Perhaps it was the future, the culture that wriggled in embryonic stages within the world as now. But perhaps it was the past, a haunting. It was a sign without a code. *How does one interpret visions? As prophecy or warning? Does fate have intention? If so, how is it discernible?* He felt sovereign, acknowledged, and his will was inspired.

Like water, questions sought the deepest recesses. They flowed into his memory and the pockets of details the decades had emptied. *Why did we live that way?* He thought from the very beginning. *If the world was so scarcely populated, why did couples only have one child?* Though then the rationale was certain—quality over quantity—now it seemed remarkably stupid. *Why abandonment and solitude?* His parents did not have to leave. They could have stayed and grown old and seen their grandson. The lessons of solitude were attainable without it.

Every detail slipped into a convention. There were so many circumstances taken as a collective given. *Was it just us?* No—it was *human*, he thought. Everyone of every age lived with rules and assumptions that eluded critical inquiry. People prayed, wore girdles, paid taxes: *did that not seem arbitrary to them?*

An odd sensation seized him; he could feel his body balanced on its halves. The duality, the symmetry: *the form of the body is like a conjoined twin*, half-father, half-mother, blended in the face, two sewn-together sacks of muscles tugged by a pair of reins in separate hemispheres of the brain.

He vomited.

*   *

He had not slept for days. Footing was shaky on the rocks in the quarry. The pace was slow. He fell to his knees, cracked a bone, and was unconscious.

The sky above was gray. Stones made a crunching noise somewhere in the direction of his feet.

They were steps. But only two: he knew what hooves sounded like. He could not move.

A shadow appeared. Above his prone body stood a person. A woman.

"What is your name?" she asked.

He heard himself say, "Mann."

She said, "We will always meet here. I have found my charge. Have you found yours?"

Silence.

"I have seen a boy," she continued, "close to manhood. You will need to provide the girl."

He was dazed.

And then we will have our revenge.

The light faded.

*   *

When he awoke, he jolted. *Was that a dream?* It felt more real than anything ever had. *Who was that woman?* She was ethereal, came from nowhere. Prevision was anchored.

She was a counsel.

The Lost Men

There was another.

It might have been a dream, but if not, life had become more sinister. His visions would burden responsibility. He must not lose himself.

Our revenge? What did that mean?

The corners frayed. He had realizations. He thought about duty, and about the roles of this secret society. Killers destroy; survivors live. *But counsels*: on the cusp of renewal, he had new knowledge, limited, like an initiate, but enough.

Was there a third species—beyond man and lost man— that lurked behind the mask of counsel: *the deceiver?* He considered it empirically. The dream of the woman was of such petty talk. Never had he seen such a human side of a counsel. She was enlisting him to hatch a scheme, which made it all fall like a house of cards.

Were counsels really clairvoyant? Those who lived had blind faith in them. But everything now seemed to disappear. *Did Joy and Paine meet clandestinely in the same way when she and I were children?* Did they hide in the bushes and spy on families and witness the solitude they suffered only to emerge vaingloriously to proclaim themselves as masters of the future? *Was it rigged?* The more he contemplated, the fuller the image grew. He channeled a spirit from the Age of Reason, a logician, a scientist. New light shone on the same factors; he was sure a rationalist could explain everything. Joy and Paine met long ago, scouted out the survivors, marked the two of them for counsel, and conducted surveillance. When they arrived years later, they knew so much about them that clairvoyance was believable. Joy would leave for months on end. *Where did she go? To a quarry like this?* Paine's closeness to Faith would be a key element to maintaining contact, for ensuring the consummation. *And the episode with the lost man? There was no evidence it ever*

David A. Colón

existed—Mann never saw the body. If Paine had known Joy long before, and had made a pact, then guiding Faith's journey across the continent to find the one, while appearing to be a stroke of divine intervention, would have been entirely feasible. *Find the boy; find the girl; pick the day, the month, the year.* Maybe the counsels had calendars, like he did. All anyone wanted to know of the future was information about the one. With this in hand, stolen from a distance, even a glib fool could feign foresight.

So what was their motive? It had to be the loss of love. He shivered at the thought of it all being a cycle. The counsels had been deceived themselves; they had once loved; love was robbed; they lost. They brought spite, anger, and vengeance to what they were themselves tricked into believing was fate. Gutting their souls made them turn to destruction, but they were not killers: they spoiled people, not consumed them.

Still, he was blind. The changes, the visions—they were real. But ask the scientist and he would tell you the pain was psychosomatic; the deformities, catatonia; the visions, hallucinations; the truth, schizophrenia. The flesh was rendered by beliefs, from within and without.

If this were all true, then the counsels had committed murder. *Boone.* He was the innocent target of their hate. Mann believed that the child was not lost. *Who knows if lost men even exist?* The geometric decrease of population could be explained by its own misguided actions and habits. *Lost men were the imagined menace that served to order society: the gaze of domination, the replacement for penal threat.*

For we all destroy. He remembered the army ants. In an eddy they poured over a mantis, chewing its eyes, tearing its limbs apart. *Is that just?* They did not seek it out: it was merely in the way. *Did they know what they*

The Lost Men

would do with it? Maybe. Were they sure they needed to consume it? Maybe. Had they thought before they acted? Maybe. It seemed more likely, though, that first they satisfied their urge to destroy, *then* applied efficiency, justification. *As do we.*

Their sin was his. He was an accomplice. He would redeem the murder of his son; he spoke a vow.

The killer, the survivor, the deceiver. They had their roles in the world of population, too. But it seemed imbalanced. *There's a harmony to life. Algebra. Al jabbar.* There had to be a fourth.

The Giver.

*   *

Blood returned to his skin. The orange trees were in bloom. Under the blue marble sky, he had a vision. A woman, not the same as the other. There was a smoking chimney.

He lay down to sleep.

*   *

Penance for his son's murder took on responsibility. *Existence is survival. Perseverance is dignity.* He grafted memories onto himself to regenerate his cells. He realized that living an individual life is more than living an individual life—it protects discourses. There are objects and language. *One ends, one doesn't.* His progeny would be his thoughts.

His sanity strengthened. He exercised his mind by reciting a lengthy mantra, of quotes and maxims, developed over time and recited often to pass the solitude. *A man's paradise is his good nature. He lived in a depth of moral isolation too remote for casual access. The wise*

David A. Colón

man hesitates before speaking about that which he does not fully understand. A decade later and the mantra took days to recite entirely. Ethics would be his pivot, to suspend the tension between panic and repose that governs our lives.

Now he saw what it meant to be a counsel: to know more than the others but to be ignored by the urges of youth. He was a eunuch; he had lost his virility, the standard of worth for the young. *But counseling is the purpose of life—to accrue wisdom through suffering and aspiration, made wisdom by virtue of imparting it to another.*

He was surprised to find himself contemplating this.

*   *

He could feel the beauty of Puget Sound. It mirrored the sky, and the squiggles of landscape and their distant colors were still and serene.

There were cities: Vancouver, Vanderhoof. In the forest, millennial redwoods towered like Gothic cathedrals. He continued to see beneath the world, the runes of possibility. He was losing himself at times but still felt whole.

Does fate equal hope? When we hope, we desire, and what we desire is what we have lacked, or needed, or become dependent on. The past is a body that dreams hope. Fate is the past. It is the root of experience that poses the questions it answers.

There was a stone bridge that crossed a stream.

He noticed he thought in terms of *we*, not *I*.

He had not forgotten the counsels. His conviction that the counsels were deceivers had loosened, forgiven. There was nothing but his will. He had developed a new vocabulary for discussing fate, one that animated the same forces but more believably, in a vernacular. Fate was his will—if he believed it, then it was fate. Fate and will would not compete.

It was no longer true that Faith had never imparted wisdom upon anyone.

He knew what he had to do now. He felt the robes of counsel enshroud him, and it was only a matter of time before he would assume his position.

She will never believe that fate is mystical. She will edify herself. She will debunk the myth of the one. She will have many, many children. She will never leave them. She will never say goodbye.

Perhaps he *would* deceive her, deceive her if necessary: deceive her into doing the good. He would stay true to the morals of the life he had lived. He would not waste the past.

He came to a clearing and saw the sign. There was a stone well, and the ground was wet in patches.

He drifted, tingling, overcome with attention. The colors were dark and strong, like the smell of the woods. Clearing led to clearing.

No, he thought. *I will not deceive her.* He changed his mind.

She will be my truth.

*   *

He came upon a house, a big log cabin. He could smell sweet smoke in the air. The feeling was familiar, extending to his childhood. A second layer of light shone down on the scene. He limped, sensing, noticing. Further back, a shed.

There was a woman: bare-chested, defined, tan, chopping wood on a stump, each short log split with a heavy stroke of her axe. He approached as she concentrated. She split another. She stood the next. It fell in halves.

Then there was a pause.

He heard the grassy thud as the axe fell by her feet.

His face was lax with recognition, and he cleared his throat to speak for the first time in a long while.

"You must be Hope."

Elsewhen Press
a small independent publisher specialising in Speculative Fiction

The Lost Men
an allegory
David Colón

In a world where the human population has been decimated, self-reliance is the order of the day. Of necessity, the few remaining people must adapt residual technology as far as possible, with knowledge gleaned from books that were rescued and have been treasured for generations. After a childhood of such training, each person is abandoned by their parents when they reach adulthood, to pursue an essentially solitary existence. For most, the only human contact is their counsel, a mentor who guides them to find 'the one', their life mate as decreed by Fate. Lack of society brings with it a lack of taboo, ensuring that the Fate envisioned by a counsel is enacted unquestioningly. The only threats to this stable, if sparse, existence are the 'lost men', mindless murderers who are also self-sufficient but with no regard for the well-being of others, living outside the confines of counsel and Fate.

Is Fate a real force, or is it totally imagined, an arbitrary convention, a product of mankind's self-destructive tendency? In this allegorical tale, David Colón uses an alternate near-future to explore the boundaries of the human condition and the extent to which we are prepared to surrender our capacity for decisions and self-determination in the face of a very personally directed and apparently benevolent, authoritarianism. Is it our responsibility to rebuke inherited 'wisdom' for the sake of envisioning and manifesting our own will?

David Colón is an Assistant Professor of English at TCU in Fort Worth, Texas, USA. Born and raised in Brooklyn, New York, he received his Ph.D. in English from Stanford University and was a Chancellor's Postdoctoral Fellow in English at the University of California, Berkeley. His writing has appeared in numerous journals, including *Cultural Critique*, *Studies in American Culture*, *DIAGRAM*, *How2*, and *MELUS*. *The Lost Men* is his first book.

ISBN: 9781908168146 (epub, kindle)
ISBN: 9781908168047 (192pp paperback)

For more information visit lost-men.com

Visit the Elsewhen Press website at elsewhen.co.uk for the latest information on all of our titles, authors and events; to read our blog; find out where to buy our books and ebooks; or to place an order.

ALSO AVAILABLE FROM

Elsewhen Press
a small independent publisher specialising in Speculative Fiction

[Re]Awakenings
AN ANTHOLOGY OF NEW SPECULATIVE FICTION
- ALISON BUCK - NEIL FAARID - GINGERLILY -
- ROBIN MORAN - PR POPE - ALEXANDER SKYE -
- PETER WOLFE -

[Re]Awakenings are the starting points for life-changing experiences; a new plane of existence, an alternate reality or cyber-reality. This genre-spanning anthology of new speculative fiction explores that theme with a spectrum of tales, from science fiction to fantasy to paranormal; in styles from clinically serious to joyfully silly. As you read through them all, and you must read all of them, you will discover along the way that stereo-typical distinctions between the genres within speculative fiction are often arbitrary and unhelpful. You will be taken on an emotional journey through a galaxy of sparkling fiction; you will laugh, you will cry; you will consider timeless truths and contemplate eternal questions.

All of life is within these pages, from birth to death (and in some cases beyond). In all of these stories, most of them specifically written for this anthology, the short story format has been used to great effect. If you haven't already heard of some of these authors, you soon will as they are undoubtedly destined to become future stars in the speculative fiction firmament. Remember, you read them here first!

[Re]Awakenings is a collection of short stories from exciting new voices in UK speculative fiction, compiled by guest editor PR Pope. It contains the following stories: Alison Buck: *Dreamers*; *Intervention*; *Mirror mirror*, *Podcast*. Neil Faarid: *The Adventures of Kit Brennan: Kidnapped!* Gingerlily: *The Dragon and the Rose*. Robin Moran: *The Merry Maiden Wails*. PR Pope: *Afterlife*; *Courtesy Bodies*; *On the Game*. Alexander Skye: *BlueWinter*; *Dreaming Mars*; *Exploring the Heavens*; *Worth it*. Peter Wolfe: *If you go into the woods today…*

ISBN: 9781908168108 (epub, kindle)
ISBN: 9781908168009 (288pp paperback)

For more information visit bit.ly/ReAwakenings

Visit the Elsewhen Press website at elsewhen.co.uk for the latest information on all of our titles, authors and events; to read our blog; find out where to buy our books and ebooks; or to place an order.

ALSO AVAILABLE FROM
Elsewhen Press
a small independent publisher specialising in Speculative Fiction

Queens of Antares
Bloodline returned
VOLUME 1 OF THE BLOODLINE TRILOGY
PR POPE

What would you do if you found out your dotty old Gran wasn't from Surrey after all, but from a planet six hundred light years away across the galaxy? Not only that, but she's really an exiled Princess from a Royal family that has been virtually wiped out by a tyrannical usurper. Would you believe it?

That's the question being asked by Caroline, Alex and Emily Wright, after moving in with Gran when their Father loses his job.

But you might find it easier to believe, if you were actually standing on that self-same planet looking into a sky with two suns.

That's the situation in which Caroline, Alex and Emily find themselves when they accidentally get transported across the galaxy.

Would you join the fight for freedom against the tyrant, if that was the only way to get back home to Earth?

You now understand the dilemma facing Caroline, Alex and Emily.

What would you do?

Queens of Antares: Bloodline is a new trilogy for readers of all ages from 10 to 100. Already compared to CS Lewis and CJ Cherryh, PR Pope weaves an enchanting tale around three young people who are accidentally transported from their mundane lives to a new world, where they must find the strength to lead a revolution in order to make their way home. On the way they discover who they really are, where they belong and the enduring power of a bloodline.

ISBN: 9781908168115 (epub, kindle)
ISBN: 9781908168016 (224pp paperback)

For more information visit www.queensofantares.co.uk

Visit the Elsewhen Press website at elsewhen.co.uk for the latest information on all of our titles, authors and events; to read our blog; find out where to buy our books and ebooks; or to place an order.

COMING SOON FROM
Elsewhen Press
a small independent publisher specialising in Speculative Fiction

LiGa™
Sanem Ozdural

Welcome.

You are hereby invited to compete in a tournament of LifeGame™ Bridge ("LiGa™ Bridge"). LiGa™ Bridge is a tournament of duplicate individual bridge in which eight players gamble with, and for, a portion of their lives.

Yes, it is possible to gamble with life! We have the technology. Life-gambling is enabled by a process we call "hand imprinting". The physical manifestation of this is a network of cranberry-hued lines on the palms of the players' left hands. These lines track the natural print of the palm and the effect is akin to a fortune-teller's hand map.

You will be gambling with a portion of your remaining life to win a portion of the other players' lives. To be precise, each player will wager one third of his/her remaining life per game, as measured by Life Points, to win one quarter of the total Life Points deposited by the losing four players. The losers' remaining lives will be shortened by one third.

The tournament ends when one – or more – of the players reaches 100 Life Points. This is the point at which the age-related degeneration of the human body ceases completely, irreversibly, and indefinitely. A somewhat misleading term that is applied to this state is 'immortality'. Reaching 100 Life Points does not mean you cannot be killed, only that you will not age. In other words, immortal does not mean invincible.

If you wish to enter the tournament you must submit a non-refundable entrance fee of $10,000,000.00.

Xavier Redd (Imm.)

Sanem Ozdural's debut slipstream novel, set in a near-future where technology to transfer the regenerative power of a body's cells from one person to another is available to a select few, provides a fascinating insight into the motivation both of those who win virtual immortality and those who will lose some of their life expectancy.

ISBN: 9781908168160 (epub, kindle) July 2012
ISBN: 9781908168061 (400pp paperback) December 2012

Visit the Elsewhen Press website at elsewhen.co.uk for the latest information on all of our titles, authors and events; to read our blog; find out where to buy our books and ebooks; or to place an order.

COMING SOON FROM
Elsewhen Press
a small independent publisher specialising in Speculative Fiction

BLUE FRIDAY
MIKE FRENCH

Dystopian science fiction, Blue Friday tells of a future where many live in fear of the Family Protection Agency, a special police division enforcing the strict legislation that has been introduced to protect the family unit. Combining dark humour with a vision of the future that is almost an inverse of the classic dystopian nightmare of 1984, the latest novel from Mike French follows in the tradition of great Speculative Fiction satirists such as Jonathan Swift.

In the Britain of Blue Friday, overtime for married couples is banned, there is enforced viewing of family television (much of it repeats of old shows from the sixties and seventies), monitored family meal-times and a coming of age where twenty-five year-olds are automatically assigned a spouse by the state computer if they have failed to marry. Only the Overtime Underground network resists.

Mike's novel is thoughtful, while at the same time prompting a wry smile in the reader. It reverses the usual dystopian vision of a future regime driven by productivity and industrial output at the expense of family, demonstrating that the converse may be no better.

Mike French is the owner and senior editor of the prestigious literary magazine, *The View From Here* which has been called many fine things since it started in 2007 including "Attractive, informative, sparkling and useful" by Iain M. Banks and for having a "great passion and drive" by Booker shortlisted Tom McCarthy. Mike's debut novel, *The Ascent of Isaac Steward* came out in 2011 and was nominated for The Galaxy National Book Awards.

ISBN: 9781908168177 (epub, kindle) September 2012
ISBN: 9781908168078 (208pp paperback) November 2012

Visit the Elsewhen Press website at elsewhen.co.uk for the latest information on all of our titles, authors and events; to read our blog; find out where to buy our books and ebooks; or to place an order.

COMING SOON FROM
Elsewhen Press
a small independent publisher specialising in Speculative Fiction

ENTANGLEMENT
DOUGLAS THOMPSON

In 2180, travel to neighbouring star systems has been mastered thanks to quantum teleportation using the 'entanglement' of sub-atomic matter; astronauts on earth can be duplicated on a remote world once the dupliport chamber has arrived there. In this way a variety of worlds can be explored, but what humanity discovers is both surprising and disturbing, enlightening and shocking. Each alternative to mankind that the astronauts find, sheds light on human shortcomings and potential while offering fresh perspectives of life on Earth. Meanwhile, at home, the lives of the astronauts and those in charge of the missions will never be the same again.

Best described as philosophical science fiction, *Entanglement* explores our assumptions about such constants as death, birth, sex and conflict, as the characters in the story explore distant worlds and the intelligent life that lives there. It is simultaneously a novel and a series of short stories: multiple worlds, each explored in a separate chapter, a separate story; every one another step on mankind's journey outwards to the stars and inwards to our own psyche. Yet the whole is much greater than the sum of the parts; the synergy of the episodes results in an overarching story arc that ultimately tells us more about ourselves than about the rest of the universe.

Douglas Thompson's short stories have appeared in a wide range of magazines and anthologies. He won the Grolsch/Herald Question of Style Award in 1989 and second prize in the Neil Gunn Writing Competition in 2007. His first book, *Ultrameta*, published in 2009, was nominated for the Edge Hill Prize, and shortlisted for the BFS Best Newcomer Award. *Entanglement* is his fifth novel.

ISBN: 9781908168153 (epub, kindle) August 2012
ISBN: 9781908168054 (288pp paperback) November 2012

Visit the Elsewhen Press website at elsewhen.co.uk for the latest information on all of our titles, authors and events; to read our blog; find out where to buy our books and ebooks; or to place an order.

About the author

David Colón is an Assistant Professor of English at TCU in Fort Worth, Texas, USA. Born and raised in Brooklyn, New York, he received his Ph.D. in English from Stanford University and was a Chancellor's Postdoctoral Fellow in English at the University of California, Berkeley. His writing has appeared in numerous journals, including *Cultural Critique*, *Studies in American Culture*, *DIAGRAM*, *How2*, and *MELUS*. *The Lost Men* is his first book.

www.ingramcontent.com/pod-product-compliance
Ingram Content Group UK Ltd.
Pitfield, Milton Keynes, MK11 3LW, UK
UKHW041410180426
11947UKWH00007B/52